BUILDING WITH BASIC

A PROGRAMMING KIT FOR KIDS

By Gayle Arthur

alpha books

A Division of Prentice Hall Computer Publishing
11711 North College Avenue, Carmel, IN 46032 USA

To my husband, Stephen, and my children, Benjamin and Ashley, for their patience and support.

International Standard Book Number: 0-672-30057-5

Library of Congress Catalog Card Number: 92-73374

95   94   93   92   8   7   6   5   4   3   2   1

Interpretation of the printing code: the rightmost number of the first series of numbers is the year of the book's printing; the rightmost number of the second series of numbers is the number of the book's printing. For example, a printing code of 92-1 shows that the first printing of the book occurred in 1992.

Printed in the United States of America

Trademarks

Screen reproductions in this book were created by means of the program Collage Plus from Inner Media, Inc., Hollis, NH.

Acknowledgments

Ashley Arthur, age 9, who thought of the Salmon Adventure and the 8-Ball Game.

Charylene Brombaugh, who is Director of the Computer Discovery Center at the Children's Museum of Indianapolis, Indiana.

Publisher
Marie Butler-Knight

Managing Editor
Elizabeth Keaffaber

Product Development Manager
Lisa A. Bucki

Children's Project Manager
Sherry Kinkoph

Development Editor
Wayne Blankenbeckler

Production Editors
Lisa C. Hoffman
Linda Hawkins

Copy Editors
Barry Childs-Helton
Howard Peirce
Audra Gable

Cover Art Director
Dan Armstrong

Cover Illustrator
April Goodman Willy

Designer
Kevin Spear

Illustrators
Mario Noche
Kevin Spear

Indexer
Hilary J. Adams

Book Production
Tim Groeling
Carrie Keesling
John Kane
Roger Morgan
Michael J. Nolan
Linda Quigley
Michelle Self
Dennis Sheehan
Greg Simsic
Kevin Spear
Angie Trzepacz
Alyssa Yesh

Special Kid Consultants
Steven Davis
Trevor Fulk
Dalila Hambrite
Rachel Parker
Nicholas Reed
Bryan Stauch
Brian Waltz
Cyrus Yamin

Special thanks to Margaret A. Colvin for ensuring the technical accuracy of this book.

CONTENTS

KIDS' INTRODUCTION

C omputers can do some pretty great stuff. Maybe you've thought about doing some
great stuff with computers yourself. Ask yourself these questions:

■ Are you curious about how computers play games, draw pictures, or make music?

■ Do you have ideas for a better computer game than any you have seen so far?

■ Are you looking for a challenge or something new to do on your computer?

If you answered *yes* to any of these questions, then you know at least one reason to learn
about computer programming. Here are some more reasons:

■ It's fun to write your own programs.

■ You can get exactly what you want from your own programs.

■ Computer programs help you learn how to make things work.

This book will show you how to use a computer language called BASIC to program your
computer to do all kinds of great stuff. You can use BASIC to make your own adventure
game with music, pictures, and animation!

By the time you are through with this book, you'll be able to figure out how to use BASIC
for your own programming ideas. But watch out! You might like BASIC so much that you
play with it in all of your spare time. You might like it better than your Nintendo.

How To Use This Book

T his book will teach you BASIC commands and what they do by showing you
programming examples from adventure games. In each chapter, you'll study a
program sample and see how each part of it works. There are also several appendixes in

the back of this book that contain a glossary of words, codes, program listings, and instructions for writing an adventure game.

As you are reading about programming, look for these special boxes throughout the book:

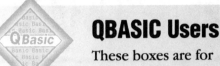

QBASIC Users

These boxes are for readers who have the QBASIC version of BASIC programming. QBASIC uses some different BASIC commands.

TechnoBabble

These boxes will have definitions of technical programming words and BASIC commands.

Try This!

These boxes will have activities for you to try on your own computer and exercises to help you learn about programming.

What's on the Disk?

The disk that came with this book contains 20 programming examples that will help you learn about BASIC. Included are programs for game stories, drawings, music, and even some animation. You'll see what these programs look like as you read through the book. The examples you study will help you learn BASIC commands. If you get really good at BASIC, you could even put some of these program examples together to make an adventure game. Or, you could use parts of these samples to create your own game.

Good Luck

The best way to learn BASIC programming is to try it yourself. Practice makes perfect! It takes longer to learn BASIC than it does to learn games and other computer activities, but if you keep at it, and are patient, learning to program your computer will get easier and easier. Get ready to have fun. Computer programming can be quite an adventure.

BASICALLY STARTING

B efore you dig into this book, you'll need to find out a few things about the computer you'll be using. You'll also need to copy the program disk that came with this book so that you will have a backup copy. *And* if your computer has a hard drive, you'll need to copy the disk onto that hard drive. Gee, that's a lot to get started! Don't worry, though. Just follow these instructions. (Have your parents or a teacher help you out.)

What You Will Need

1 ▶ First of all, make sure you are working with an IBM or IBM-compatible computer.

2 ▶ Your computer should have DOS 2.1 or a more recent version. (DOS, a Disk Operating System, is a popular program that helps run your computer.)

3 ▶ And finally, your computer should have one of the following BASIC program versions. (You'll learn what BASIC is in Chapter 2.)

- QBASIC
- GWBASIC
- BASIC
- BASICA

Does Your Computer Have BASIC?

Most computers already have one of these BASIC programs installed. Here's how to find out what version you have. Turn on your computer and wait for the DOS prompt to appear. It will look like this:

```
C:>   or   A:>
```

Now you need to make your computer list the programs it has stored. Type this command right after the DOS prompt:

```
DIR/W
```

The computer will show you a list of programs and files in your computer. Read the list and look for your computer's version of BASIC. If you have BASIC, it will be in one of these file names:

> BASIC.EXE
>
> GWBASIC.EXE
>
> BASICA.EXE
>
> QBASIC.EXE

Did you find one of these names? If you're having trouble finding your version of BASIC, ask your parents or a teacher to help. Your version might be in a directory where you can't see it. Have someone help you look in the directories on your computer. (A directory is a storage area in your computer where you can put files and keep them organized.)

If you found it, that's great! You'll know which type of BASIC you have.

Now you need to copy the program disk. Follow the directions in this next section.

Copying the Program Disk

When you are making a copy of the program disk, follow exactly the directions listed here. Do not put spaces between words or letters unless shown. Make sure you have a 5¼-inch, double-density floppy disk to copy the *Building with BASIC* disk to. (Have your parents or a teacher help you with this.)

Follow these steps to make a copy of the *Building with BASIC* disk:

1 ▸ Start your computer.

2 ▸ On the keyboard type `DISKCOPY A: A:` or `DISKCOPY B: B:` (depending on the drive in which you placed the disk) and then press `Enter`.

3 ▸ Carefully follow the prompts that appear on-screen, inserting the *source* (*Building with BASIC*) and *target* (blank) disks when asked to. You will see messages like

```
Insert SOURCE disk in drive A (or B)
and press any key...

  or

Insert TARGET disk in drive A (or B)
and press any key...
```

4 ▸ When the disk copying process is complete, the instructions on-screen will read

```
Copy another diskette?  (Y/N)
```

Type `N` to finish copying the *Building with BASIC* disk.

5 ▸ Store your original copy of the *Building with BASIC* disk for safekeeping.

In case you didn't know. . . .

A floppy disk stores programs and information that you want to keep. It's kind of like recording your favorite TV show or song onto a video tape or cassette tape. A floppy disk works the same way. There are two kinds of floppy disks, a 5$\frac{1}{4}$-inch size and a 3$\frac{1}{2}$-inch size. The disk that came with this book is a 5$\frac{1}{4}$-inch disk. Floppy disks slide into the floppy disk drive slot on the front of your computer.

Installing the Programs on a Hard Drive

If your computer has a hard drive, you'll probably want to copy the disk programs to your hard drive. The following procedure shows you how to copy the *Building with BASIC* program files to a directory you create on your hard drive:

1. Make sure that you have booted up the computer with DOS in the usual fashion. You'll need to be at the DOS prompt (C:>) before you continue with this procedure.

2. Make sure you are in the root directory. Type CD\ and then press Enter.

3. Make a directory named BWB on your hard drive. This is the place where all of your files will reside. Type MD\BWB and then press Enter.

4. Change your directory to the subdirectory that will contain the *Building with BASIC* program files. Type CD\BWB and then press Enter.

5. Place your copied *Building with BASIC* disk in drive A or B.

6. Copy the *Building with BASIC* files to the BWB subdirectory on the hard disk. Type COPY A:*.* or COPY B:*.* and then press Enter.

7. To run BASIC from the hard drive, type the name of your version of BASIC (QBASIC, GWBASIC, BASIC or BASICA) and then press Enter.

8. If this does not work, you may need to change this command to include the directory where your BASIC program is stored. For example, if you have GWBASIC and the program is stored in the DOS directory, you would type \DOS\GWBASIC and then press Enter.

Okay, Now You're Ready

If you've found what version of BASIC you have and copied the program disk, then you're all ready to go!

CHAPTER ONE
WHAT MAKES A COMPUTER?

It's a boat anchor, it's modern art, it's an end table . . . no—it's a computer!

Q: What's the difference between a computer and a big plastic box filled with metal and glass?

A: Keep reading and you'll find out. (Hint: It starts with a *p*.)

How Does a Computer Know What to Do?

A **computer program** is a set of instructions that tells a computer what to do. Sounds simple enough.

Without a program, though, a computer is the world's most expensive dust catcher. Playing with a computer without a program would be like using your VCR to watch a movie without a tape inside.

Some of the computers you've seen before *seem* smart, but a computer can't figure things out like a person can. It can't even make a guess!

Computer instructions have to be very specific and detailed. The program cannot leave anything to the computer's imagination, because a computer doesn't have an imagination. A computer has no common sense, either. A computer will not do any task unless you tell it to.

If you go to the store to buy a game for your computer, you are really buying a computer program. The program was created by a **computer programmer**.

TechnoBabble

A **computer programmer** is a person who knows how to write instructions the computer can understand. A **computer program** is a set of instructions that tells the computer what to do.

What Is a Computer Language?

Now that you know that computers aren't so smart without a program, think about this:

Imagine that you want to give a friend directions to your house. Would the directions you write for your friend be the same as directions you would write for a computer?

The biggest difference between writing a computer program and writing directions for a friend is the language you use. You see, computers don't understand English—computers only understand **machine language.**

This is what machine language for a computer might look like:

```
01011001      11011101      00010001      10101101

00011100      01110001      10111110      01101100
```

If the thought of writing instructions that look like this does not excite you, don't worry. You're not going to have to do that. There's an easier way. Writing a program in machine language would be a real pain.

That's why there are **computer programming languages**. A programming language like BASIC is a lot easier for most people to learn than machine language.

Programming languages translate your English-language instructions into something the computer will understand.

PASCAL, FORTRAN, and COBOL are some other programming languages that are used.

So What Does a Program Do Anyway?

Each computer program has a special job to do—it has a

purpose or use. The job it does is called its **application**. But if you want a computer to do a job, first you have to tell it how—step by step. That means you'd better have a pretty good idea of how to do that job.

Programming is like teaching the computer to do something you know how to do. If you want to enter a secret family recipe in a magazine's cooking contest, you must know how to make the dish yourself. Before you can draw a map to your house, you must know how to get there yourself.

In the same way, computer programmers must know what the computer program will be used for—its special job—before they can write down all the instructions the computer will need.

TechnoBabble

Machine language is the language that a computer understands. It uses strange-looking words, and it requires many instructions for even a simple task.

Programming languages translate your instructions into something the computer will understand.

Every computer program has a job to do. An **application** is what programmers call that job.

Before they start writing a program, smart programmers do a lot of research to learn everything they can about what they want to program. A programmer tries to know everything about the use for the program. That way he or she won't leave out important parts when it's time to write down all those computer instructions.

Computer programs have been written for many applications, including:

- Playing games.
- Working with words.
- Drawing.

- Making music.
- Working with facts and lists.
- Working with numbers.

These applications turn a computer into a very useful tool. You've probably used some of these programs at home or at your school.

Types of Programs

You probably know all about computer games. They're a blast. But did you know that each one is actually a program?

Have you ever typed a report or a letter on a computer? You were using a word processing program. Once you get used to typing on a keyboard, these programs make it easy to get your reports to come out looking good.

Drawing programs let you draw pictures with a computer. Sometimes the pictures are neater than anything you could draw yourself. You can even mess around with pictures that someone else made up.

Computers can even play music. Music programs can tell the computer when to make each sound, so that they come out like musical notes.

With a database program that keeps track of lists, you could organize your baseball card collection. For each card, you can let your computer keep track of the player's name, what year the card was made, and how much you paid for the card.

Some programs are fine for working with numbers and math. If you have a job as a newspaper carrier, you could use one of these programs to keep track of the money you can make. This type of program turns your computer into a fancy "calculator, pencil, and paper." They're called spreadsheet programs.

You should try using programs like this when you get a chance. Try to find a lot of different ways to use them.

There are lots of other good ideas for applications beside the ones we've talked about. The list could go on and on and on.

How Do You Make a Computer Program?

Suppose you know of an application that you want to program. You know everything you need to know about its use. Now you must write down all the instructions for the computer.

These instructions must be in the right order. And the instructions must be very clear. Remember, computers aren't very smart—they just do what you tell them to do.

Try This!

Think up some more jobs your computer can do. Make a list of five silly applications. Make a list of five serious applications.

For example, some silly uses might be:

- Program embarrassing sounds.
- Program your computer to make your bed.
- Program your computer to put air in your bicycle tires whenever they get flat.

Some examples of serious uses:

- List and organize video tapes.
- Make a newsletter for your club.
- Write letters to your grandparents.
- Keep track of the money you make babysitting.

Are Computers Really That Dumb Without a Program?

Look at the next example of two "programs." Program 1 and Program 2 are both instructions for making a peanut-butter sandwich. One of the programs is for a computer robot, the other is for your friend. Can you guess which is which?

Program 1

```
1.  Put the peanut butter on the bread.
```

Program 2

```
1.  Unscrew the lid from a jar of peanut butter.
2.  Open a sack of bread.
3.  Remove a slice of bread.
4.  Get a knife.
5.  Place the knife in the peanut butter.
6.  Scoop out some peanut butter using the knife.
7.  Spread the peanut butter from the knife onto the
    slice of bread.
8.  Remove another slice of bread from the sack.
9.  Put the second slice of bread on top of the first
    slice of bread.
10. Eat the sandwich!
```

Do you see that the instructions in Program 2 are in the correct order? What would happen if the steps were in a different order? Could you do step 5 before step 4? In other words, could you place the knife in the peanut butter before you told the computer to get a knife? The computer would not know how to handle these mixed-up instructions.

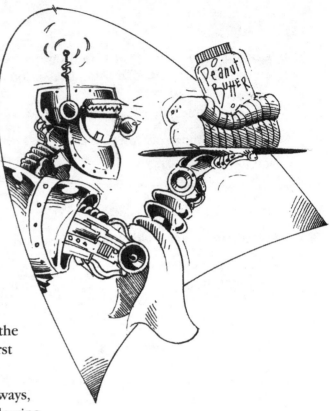

Clear as a Bell

You've got to make your computer instructions really clear. Do you think the robot will know how to place the bread slices in step 9? How would the robot know that it's supposed to place the second slice on the gooey side of the first slice?

If the robot put the slices together sideways, would the robot be wrong? No. Just following orders!

Program 2 has more details for the computer robot, but what would the robot do with Program 1? Well . . . remember, computers have no common sense.

Program 1 is clear enough for your human friend. Most kids have enough common sense to take the lid off the jar! What would your friend think if you gave him or her directions like Program 2?

Not only do you have to make your computer instructions clear, but you also have to write them in a computer language that the machine will understand. In the next chapter, you'll learn about a computer language called BASIC.

Try This!

This activity will show you why it's so important to put the steps of a program in the right order.

Here are some mixed-up steps for putting on your shoes and socks:

___ Tie a bow in the right shoelace.　　___ Find two socks.
___ Put your left foot in the left shoe.　___ Put the right sock on.
___ Make sure the socks match.　　　　___ Make sure the socks don't smell bad.
___ Put your right foot in the right shoe.　___ Tie a bow in the left shoelace.
___ Pull the laces tight on the right shoe.　___ Put the left sock on.
___ Find your shoe.　　　　　　　　___ Pull the laces tight on the left shoe.
___ You're all done.

Start with the first step you would do, and put the steps in order.

What would happen if you did these steps out of order? What would happen if you left out a step?

To Make a Long Story Short . . .

Now you know a bit more about computer programming. You know that a computer program is a set of instructions that can be understood by a computer. These instructions must be clear and in step-by-step order.

Computers understand *only* machine language; most people don't understand machine language. A computer programmer can translate English-language instructions into a computer programming language. A programming language can translate instructions into machine language for the computer.

You also learned some applications, or uses, for a computer program.

There are a lot of computer programming languages. To learn more about one of them, move on to Chapter 2.

CHAPTER TWO

THE BASICS OF BASIC

It is a warm summer evening as you sit in your backyard. You hope to get a glimpse of a shooting star. A blinding flash lights up the yard. "That was some shooting star," you think. But wait, you see a glow behind the garage. "Wow, maybe it's a meteorite. Check it out!"

You follow the glow. You hear a humming noise. When you turn the corner of the garage you see a strange thing hovering over the roof, slowly descending toward the lawn. "Is it a meteor, a spaceship, a bad dream?" You must decide whether to investigate this matter, go on to bed, or call 911!

D o you like adventure stories and games? This eerie story is just an example of an adventure game you can build on your computer. You can use BASIC programming language to program adventures like this one, but first you need to know more about BASIC.

BASIC Background

T here are several different versions of the BASIC programming language. BASIC has been around for 30 years in one form or another—and it came free with most of the home computers right out of their boxes.

BASIC Basics

BASIC actually stands for **B**eginner's **A**ll-Purpose **S**ymbolic **I**nstruction **C**ode. Sounds scary, doesn't it? Just remember that BASIC is a special language that tells a computer what to do.

Remember how we told a robot computer to make a peanut butter sandwich in Chapter 1? All the instructions were in order. That's the way BASIC works—it uses lines of ordered commands to program your computer.

There are two main types of BASIC—"regular" BASIC and QBASIC. GWBASIC, BASIC, and BASICA are what we'll call "regular" BASIC. These three versions are almost exactly alike.

QBASIC is a new and improved version. On your computer screen, QBASIC will look very different from regular BASIC. It also has many slick, new features that make BASIC easier and more powerful.

But it does not matter which version of BASIC you're using. The instructions in this book will usually work with any version.

Sometimes a command may work a little different in QBASIC. If you have this version, be on the lookout for the **QBASIC Users** boxes throughout the book. They will explain some special ways that QBASIC works.

The rest of this chapter is divided into two parts—one is for "regular" BASIC users, the other is for QBASIC users. QBASIC users won't want to read about how to use "regular" BASIC. And the QBASIC section will look weird to users of "regular" BASIC.

The next section is only for "regular" BASIC users (GWBASIC, BASIC, BASICA). So, QBASIC users should skip ahead to the section called "For QBASIC Users Only." "Regular" BASIC users—it's time to get started!

GWBASIC, BASIC, and BASICA Users

You can start "regular" BASIC just like you start any other computer program. You type in GWBASIC, BASIC, or BASICA—just as it was spelled when you looked for your version on your computer in the introduction— and press Enter. If everything is working, your version of BASIC will show up on your screen (that means the BASIC program is in your computer's memory) so you can now play with it. If BASIC does not come up on your screen, you should get help from a parent or someone who knows about computers.

Once you have started BASIC, your computer screen should look like this picture:

This area reminds you what the shortcut "F" keys are for.

```
The COMPAQ Personal Computer BASIC
Version 3.31

(C) Copyright Compaq Computer Corp. 1982, 1988
(C) Copyright Microsoft Corp. 1983, 1987
60133 Bytes free
Ok
```

```
1LIST  2RUN←  3LOAD"  4SAVE"  5CONT←  6,"LPT1  7TRON←  8TROFF←  9KEY   0SCREEN
```

This is what you'll see when you start up BASIC.

At the top of the screen you will see a lot of information about your version of BASIC, and about the company that makes BASIC, Microsoft.

The next line says OK. That tells you everything is all right with BASIC, and it is your turn to type something in where the cursor is blinking.

The words across the bottom are there to remind you of some shortcut keys—the **F keys**—and to tell you which ones to press. These are BASIC words you will be using a lot; the

F keys save you a little bit of time—and they don't make typing errors. In this chapter you will learn about the F keys you'll be using most.

Let's Get Runnin' . . .

Let's start learning about BASIC by typing a BASIC program.

Your screen should still show the OK and blinking cursor. Just type in the following lines. Press the Enter key at the end of each line. Lines of computer instruction are called **statements**. (Be careful as you type. Try to make your new program look just like this one, including the numbers and the spaces.)

```
1 REM Program FIRST.BAS This is your first program
2 INPUT "What is your name? ", FIRSTNAME$
3 PRINT "Thanks for playing, ", FIRSTNAME$, "I hope you had fun!"
4 END
```

What have you done? Well, you just typed in four BASIC statements. (The number at the beginning of each line tells the computer to store that line in the computer's memory. We'll learn more about what programming lines are used for in the next chapter.)

Right now, your computer screen should look like this:

```
The COMPAQ Personal Computer BASIC
Version 3.31

(C) Copyright Compaq Computer Corp. 1982, 1988
(C) Copyright Microsoft Corp. 1983, 1987
60133 Bytes free
Ok



1 REM Program FIRST.BAS This is your first program
2 INPUT "What is your name? ", FIRSTNAME$
3 PRINT "Thanks for playing, ", FIRSTNAME$, "I hope you had fun!"
4 END






1LIST  2RUN←  3LOAD"  4SAVE"  5CONT←  6,"LPT1 7TRON← 8TROFF← 9KEY  0SCREEN
```

Your screen should look like this after you type in the first sample program lines.

If you want to see what this program does, you have to **RUN** it. Type in the word RUN and press Enter, or you can press the F2 key (that's the shortcut). Try this to see what the program does. When the program asks you "What is your name?" type in your name and press Enter.

Save Your First Program!

So far, you typed a BASIC program, and it's still in your computer's memory. Now let's give the program a name, and save it on a disk. Program names can only be eight characters long.

You'll want to save most of your programs on a disk, because then you can use each one whenever you want. If you save a program on a disk, it's always there for you—you won't have to type in all the statements every time you want to see it.

The next activity shows you how to save your program on a disk.

Try This!

Let's name your program and save it all at the same time. Type this on your screen.

```
SAVE"FIRST"
```

Then press the Enter key. You just saved your program and named it FIRST.BAS. All BASIC programs have the letters BAS after the period, even if you don't add it yourself to the program's name.

If you want to save the program on a disk in another disk drive, be sure to name the disk drive letter, like this:

```
SAVE"B:FIRST"
```

for the B: floppy disk drive, then press Enter.

You can be sure your program is saved when you save it on a disk. But just to prove it, you can erase the progam from your computer's current memory, and then reload it from the disk where you just saved the program. Try the next activity—but follow directions carefully!

Try This!

First, erase the computer's current memory. Type this:

```
NEW
```

And press Enter. Now, we'll try to RUN a program. Type this:

```
RUN
```

And press Enter. Nothing happens, right? Your program isn't in the memory anymore—but the program *is* on the disk, because we saved it before we typed in NEW.

WARNING: Be careful with the **NEW** command! It wipes out programs from the computer's memory, so be sure to save any programs you want to keep before typing NEW.

Then Try This!

You can load the program called FIRST.BAS that we saved in the last activity. Type this:

```
LOAD"FIRST"
```

and then press the Enter key. If you spelled the name of the program correctly, and if the computer finds that program on the disk, the screen will show this message:

```
Ok
```

You don't have to type in the .BAS after the word "FIRST" because BASIC knows you mean a BASIC program.

A shortcut for typing the word **LOAD** is to press the F3 key.

Now your program called FIRST.BAS is in your computer's current memory. To prove it, try to RUN it! Type the word RUN and press Enter to start the program again.

Tip Offs

You should always save any program before you finish working with it.

If you want a shortcut for typing the word SAVE, press the F4 key.

TechnoBabble

The **SAVE** command is used to save your program (or other information you've typed into the computer) onto a disk or the hard drive.

The **NEW** command starts a fresh program. But be careful using this command. It wipes out programs from the computer's memory—unless they're saved!

What If I Make a Mistake Typing In the Program?

No problem! BASIC has certain rules about spelling and punctuation. Whenever you make a mistake and run the program, you will get a message telling you something isn't correct. The message will point out the line where the mistake is. Nice, huh? All you have to do is put the cursor over the mistake, and then type over it to correct it. This is called **editing**.

Want to see what happens when your program has an error? Try this next activity.

Try This!

Start by typing in a mistake—on purpose—in a BASIC statement. Type in this little program, just the way it is here. Let's just see what happens.

```
1 REM Program SECOND.BAS This program has an error
2 INPUT "What is your name ? "FIRSTNAME$
3 PRINT "Thanks for playing, " FIRSTNAME$ "I Hope you had fun!
4 END
```

When you RUN this program, your screen will show you an error message like the one you see in the picture. (Type RUN and press Enter.)

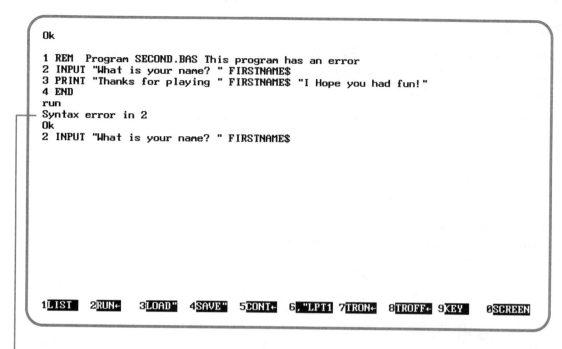

```
Ok

1 REM  Program SECOND.BAS This program has an error
2 INPUT "What is your name? " FIRSTNAME$
3 PRINT "Thanks for playing " FIRSTNAME$ "I Hope you had fun!"
4 END
run
Syntax error in 2
Ok
2 INPUT "What is your name? " FIRSTNAME$




1LIST   2RUN←   3LOAD"   4SAVE"   5CONT←   6,"LPT1  7TRON←  8TROFF←  9KEY    0SCREEN
```

Error messages like this one tell you something is wrong.

You'll see an error message like this when your program doesn't run correctly.

The error message tells you that your program has an error in punctuation or spelling.

In the activity you just tried, you left out the comma when you typed line 2 . The computer screen shows you that something is wrong with line 2.

Here is how you correct the problem.

1 Use the arrow keys on the keyboard to place the cursor right under the F in FIRSTNAME$ in line 2.

2 Press the Insert key once, because you should insert a comma and a space.

3 After you type in the comma and an empty space, press the Enter key. (If you don't press Enter while the cursor is still in the right place to correct the mistake, your correction won't happen.)

Try to RUN this program again to see if the error message prints out. It shouldn't, if you did the example just the way it is in the book.

Show Me!

Sometimes you may want to look at your BASIC program even if there is nothing wrong with the way it works. Or you might want to change something. To do this, you have to give the computer a LIST command.

The computer will list each line of the program on your computer screen. When you want to show the entire program, type:

```
LIST
```

Then press Enter.

That tells the computer to show you all the lines of the program. (A shortcut key is F1. If you press F1, the word LIST prints on your computer screen. Then you just press the Enter key.)

Tip Offs

What if you want to take your program listing away from the computer to study it? You can do this with the **LLIST** command. It prints out your program on your computer's printer. Just type in **LLIST** and press Enter.

If the program is very long, it will move across your screen too quickly to read it. To stop it, press the Pause key on your keyboard. If you don't have a Pause key on your keyboard, there's another way to stop the screen. While you hold down the Ctrl key, press the S key. To make it move again, press any key on the keyboard.

If you want to end the LIST before it is finished, press two keys—Ctrl and Break—and then Enter. That stops the LIST command.

You can also list part of the program. Just tell the computer which lines to LIST (don't forget the line numbers). Try this out in the next activity.

Don't Show Me!

If you want to clear your screen and make it blank, use the **CLS** command. (That stands for **CL**ear the **S**creen.) Using CLS is like using a clean sheet of paper from a notebook. It is a good idea to clear the screen before you start a new activity in your program. Just type CLS and press Enter. The CLS command doesn't erase the program from the computer's current memory or disk. It just gives you a blank computer screen.

Try This!

Let's play with the LIST command. If you want to list line number 1 *only,* type this:

```
LIST 1
```

List lines 1, 2, and 3, type this:

```
LIST 1-3
```

Now, list all the lines from 1 on to the end of the program, like this:

```
LIST 1-
```

Now, list all the lines that come before line 2, like this:

```
LIST -2
```

How to Make a Change in Your Program

It's easy to erase things you don't want in your program. Use the arrow keys to place the cursor over the letters you don't want—and then press the Delete key to erase each letter you don't need.

Another way to erase words is to use the Backspace key. The Backspace key backs up the cursor to the left and wipes out everything as it goes.

TechnoBabble

The **LIST** command shows your program lines on the computer screen. The **LLIST** command lets you print out your program on your computer's printer. The **CLS** command will clear your computer screen.

You can also type over words if you want. Whatever you type goes right on top of what was there—and takes its place.

If you want to insert words, press the Ins key. Then when you type, everything to the right of the cursor will scoot over to make room for your new words.

If you want to change just one line, just type in the line number, retype the entire line, and then press the Enter key. If you use a line number that is already in the program, the new line number will wipe out the old one. Pretty easy, huh?

What If You Want to Add a Line?

You'll notice that program lines in this book are numbered. That's because "regular" BASIC requires you to number each line of instructions so that the computer will know when to follow it. (QBASIC users don't need to number lines.) You'll also notice that some lines are numbered by tens. That's a trick programmers use to allow themselves room for extra lines, in case they want to add more instructions later.

If you want to add a line to a program, just type in the new line number and the statement, like this:

```
5 PRINT " This is fun"
6 PRINT " No Duh!"
4 PRINT " Where's the pizza?
I'm hungry."
```

Tip Offs

Here is a shortcut for changing one line. **LIST** the line you want to change. When that line is on the screen, use the arrow keys to move the cursor to the place under any letter or number you want to change. Then type over each word on a line until it looks the way you want it to look. While the cursor is still on the line you want to change, press Enter. The Enter key makes the change stick. (If you change your mind about the change, just don't press the Enter key—use the arrow keys to move off the line.)

(Don't worry. We'll learn about the PRINT command later.)

As you type in line numbers, BASIC adds them in the right place in the program—just the way you type it. Make sure you type the line numbers correctly. It's easy to make a mistake.

What would happen if you typed a 4 instead of a 4000? BASIC would place that line near the beginning of the program instead of following line 3999 where it's supposed to go.

Here's another way to add a line. (This is good if you are going to add a bunch of lines all at one time.) Type AUTO and then press Enter.

This command will print out the line numbers automatically—starting at 10. You just type what you want on each line. When you're done with a line, press Enter. The next line number pops up, and you can type what you want on that line.

AUTO uses numbers by 10, automatically—like this:

```
10
20
30
```

To make the lines increase automatically by 10 0, type `AUTO 100`.

To make the lines increase automatically by 1, type `AUTO 1`.

TechnoBabble

The **AUTO** command automatically numbers your program lines for you. (It numbers them by tens unless you tell it differently.)

What If You Want to Take Out a Line?

You may want to take out some lines in your BASIC program. The DELETE command will knock out one line or many.

The next activity will show you how to use the DELETE command.

Tip Offs

If you make any changes in your BASIC program and you want them to stay, be sure to SAVE your program when you're done changing it. Here's why. Any time you change any information in a program—and you're doing that when you add or delete lines—you'll see the change on your screen. But that only means your changes are in your computer's current memory. They won't stay unless you SAVE the program on your disk. Yikes!

Try This!

Let's delete a line from the program FIRST.BAS. (It's probably still in your computer's memory if you did the last activity.) First, list the program. Type this:

```
LIST
```

then press Enter (or press the F1 key for a shortcut).
Let's take out line 4. To do that, type this:

```
DELETE 4
```

Now list the program again. Line 4 should be gone from your program.

This is the end of the information for users of GWBASIC, BASIC, or BASICA. If your computer has one of these versions, you can skip ahead to the section called "A Bit of Advice."

For QBASIC Users Only

You start QBASIC just as you start any other computer program. You type QBASIC and press Enter. If everything is working, QBASIC will show up on your screen. This means that the BASIC program is in your computer's memory.

If QBASIC does not come up on your screen, you should get help from a parent or someone who knows about computers.

Once you have started QBASIC, the first screen you will see looks like this:

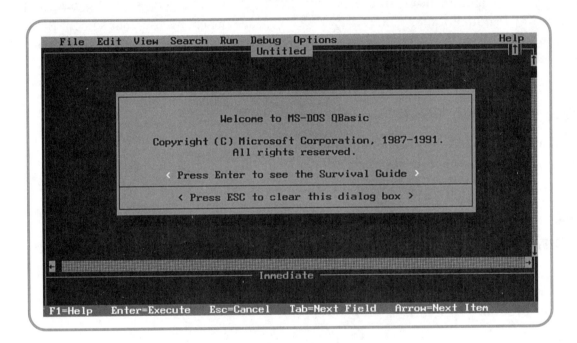

You will see this screen every time you start QBASIC.

If you press the Enter key, you can get some built-in directions called HELP to show on your screen. If you're ready to type in your new BASIC program, you can just press the Esc key to get your screen ready to go to work.

QBASIC lets you type in your BASIC program lines, just the way you would if you were using a word processor. This is a big improvement over the old versions of BASIC. Here's how the screen should look when it's ready for you to type in your BASIC commands:

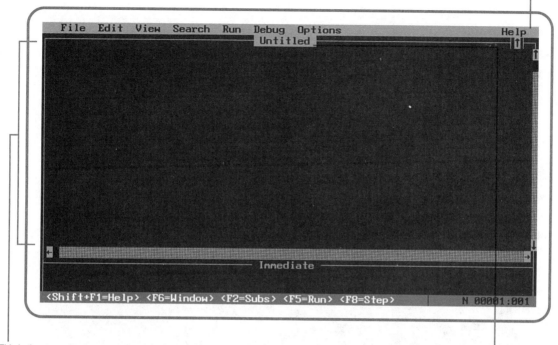

File Edit View Search Run Debug Options   Help
                              Untitled

                              Immediate

<Shift+F1=Help> <F6=Window> <F2=Subs> <F5=Run> <F8=Step>   N 00001:001

This is the area where you type in and edit your program.

The name you give a program will appear here.

This is what shows up on your computer screen when you are ready to go to work!

Tip Offs

You should take a look at the Help that QBASIC can show you on your screen (old versions of BASIC don't have Help), and it's a big improvement!

TechnoBabble

Have you ever used a pull down roller type of window shade? When you want to use it, you pull the shade down, and when you don't need it anymore, you raise it and it rolls up and out of sight. That's how a **pull-down menu** on a computer program works. You pull it down to pick choices, and then it "moves" out of the way when you're done.

QBASIC also gives you a new way to use the BASIC commands. In the old versions of BASIC, you always type in your commands. QBASIC lets you use the **pull-down menus** for some of them. It's a big difference—and a lot easier.

Let's Get Runnin' . . .

Let's start learning about QBASIC by typing a BASIC program.

Your screen should still show the OK and blinking cursor. Just type in the following lines. Press the Enter key at the end of each line. Be careful as you type. Try to make your new program look just like this one. (Don't forget to type in the numbers and the spaces.)

```
1 REM Program FIRST.BAS This is your first program
2 INPUT "What is your name? ", FIRSTNAME$
3 PRINT "Thanks for playing, ", FIRSTNAME$, "I hope you had fun!"
4 END
```

What have you done? Well, you just typed in four BASIC statements. At the beginning of each statement, you put a line number that tells the computer to store that line in the computer's memory until you run (or start) the program later. (We'll learn more about what lines are used for in the next chapter.)

Right now, your computer screen looks like this:

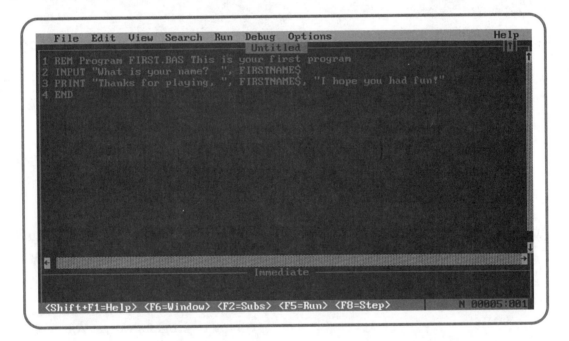

These are the four lines of the sample program.

If you want to see what this program does, you have to RUN it. You can use the pull-down menus to do this.

You can see a list of pull-down menus on the **menu bar** across the top of the screen. To make a choice, hold down the Alt key and type the first letter of the menu item you want. To run a program, for example, hold down Alt while you press R. Your screen will then look like this:

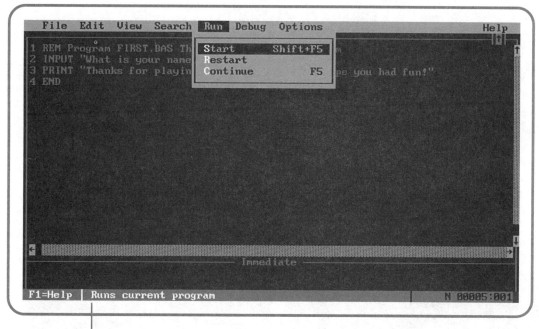

This reminds you what the menu item you've picked does.

The Run pull-down menu.

Use the arrow keys to move to the word Start (you'll see a highlight around it), then press Enter. Try running this sample program!

Save Your First Program!

So far, you typed a BASIC program, and it's still in your computer's memory. Now let's give the program a name, and save it on a disk. Program names can only be eight characters long.

TechnoBabble

The **RUN** command tells the computer that you want to see a program work. Hold down the Alt key and press R, then press S for start.

A **statement** is another name for a line in a program that has a line number, a blank space, and then a command.

You'll want to save most of your programs on a disk, because then you can use each one whenever you want. If you save a program on a disk, it's always there for you—you won't have to type in all of its statements every time you want to see it.

The next activity shows you how to save your program on a computer disk.

Try This!

Hold down the Alt key, then press the F key. That pulls down the File menu. Use the arrow keys to highlight the word Save. Press Enter again to pick Save. Now you get to type in the name of your program. For this example, type in `FIRST.BAS`. It doesn't matter whether you use upper- or lowercase letters. Your screen should look like this:

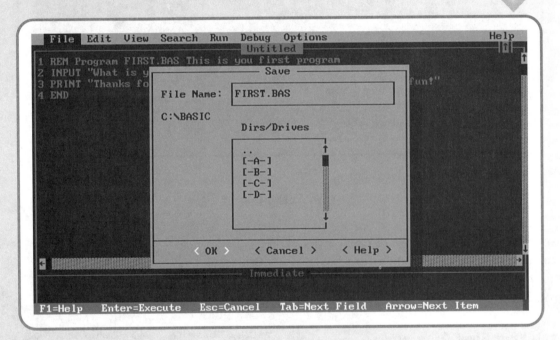

When you first save a program, you must type in a name for it.

Now press Enter. Your program is saved on a disk. Notice that FIRST.BAS shows up in a box right under the menu bar. If your program already has a name, QBASIC saves it automatically with the same name. You won't need to retype it.

Tip Offs

You don't have to use the menu to run a program—there is a shortcut. You can hold down two keys at the same time: Shift and F5.

You should always save any program before you finish working with it.

TechnoBabble

The **SAVE** command is used to save your program (or other information you've typed into the computer) onto a disk or the hard drive.

The **NEW** command clears your screen and erases it from the computer's memory.

You can be sure your program is saved when you save it on a disk. But just to prove it, you can erase the progam from your computer's current memory, and then reload it from the disk you just saved the program on.

Try the next two activities—but remember to follow directions carefully!

Try This!

We will erase the computer's current memory. Press the Alt key and then press F. That pulls down the File menu. Use the arrow keys to highlight the word New, and then press Enter. The command New erases the computer's current memory.

Let's see what happens if we try to run the program.

Hold down the Shift key while you press the F5 key. That's the shortcut to run a program. Nothing happens, right? Your program isn't in the current memory anymore, but the program is still on a disk because you saved it before you selected the New command.

WARNING: Be careful with the New command—it wipes out the computer's memory! Before you choose New from the File menu, be sure to save any programs you've written or changed.

Try This!

Let's load the program called FIRST.BAS that you saved earlier.
You use the File pull-down menu and select the Open command.
To do that, press the Alt key, and then press Enter. Then highlight
the word Open. Press Enter and the screen will look like this:

You can type in the name of the program you want to load.

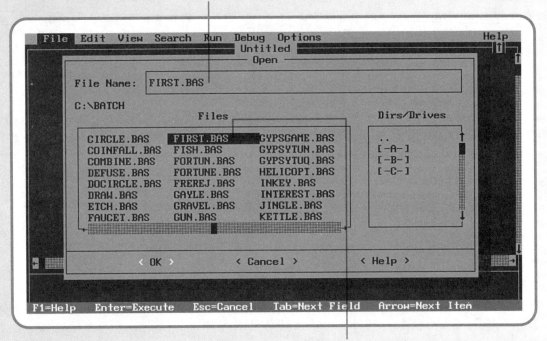

You can highlight the name of the program you want to load.

This is what the screen will look like when you want to open a program file.

You can type in the name of the program. You can also use the Tab key to move
down to a box that shows a list of programs, and then select the one you want—use
the arrow keys to highlight the name of the program, and then press Enter.

What If I Make a Mistake Typing In the Program?

No problem. QBASIC has certain rules about spelling and punctuation. When you make a mistake and run the program, you will get a message telling you something isn't correct. The message will point out the line where the mistake is. Nice, huh? All you have to do is put the cursor over the mistake, and then type over it to correct it. This is called **editing**.

Want to see what happens when your program has an error? Try this next activity.

Try This!

Start by typing in a mistake—on purpose! Type in this little program, just the way it is here. Let's just see what happens.

```
1 REM Program SECOND.BAS This program has an error
2 INPUT "What is your name ? "FIRSTNAME$
3 PRINT "Thanks for playing, " FIRSTNAME$ "I Hope you had fun!
4 END
```

QBASIC won't even let you finish entering line 2. You'll see an error message that looks like this:

The part of the program with an error is highlighted.

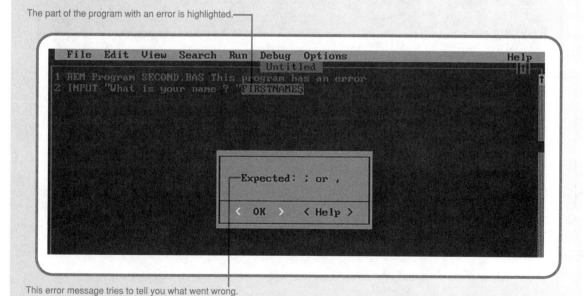

This error message tries to tell you what went wrong.

This error message tells you that something is missing that needs to be there.

In this example, you left out the comma when you typed line 2. The computer screen shows you that something is wrong with line 2.

- If you know what the problem is, press Enter—this selects OK. Then you can go ahead and type in the correction.

- If you don't know yet what the problem is, use HELP. Press the Tab key to move over to the word Help, and press Enter.

Here is what the HELP box for error messages looks like. It tells you the problem could be punctuation. To leave the HELP screen and get back to your program, press the Esc key twice. Presto! You're back.

QBASIC has help boxes that give you a lot of good information about how to use QBASIC. Whenever you want more information about QBASIC, press the Alt key and then press H. That gives you the pull-down menu.

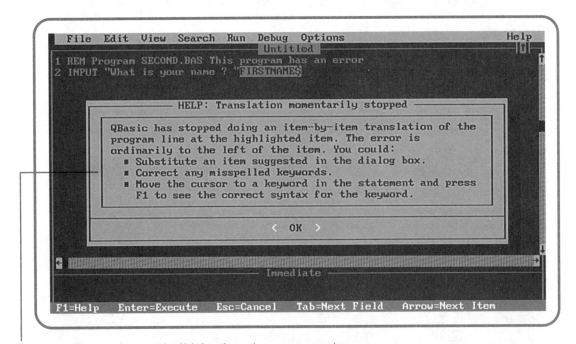

This information appears when you select Help form the previous error message box.

This is what the Help box for error messages looks like.

Here is how you correct the mistake you typed.

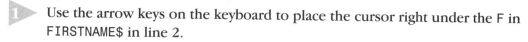

1. Use the arrow keys on the keyboard to place the cursor right under the F in FIRSTNAME$ in line 2.

2. Type a comma (,) and press the space bar (the long bar at the bottom of your keyboard). That scoots the word over to the right. This is called "inserting" a comma.

Finish typing the program, and run it—hold down the Shift key and press the F5 key. The error message shouldn't print out if you did the example just the way it is in the book.

How to Make a Change in Your Program

When you type words on a QBASIC line, you *insert* words—everything else in a QBASIC line "scoots over" to the right to make room for what you type. Sometimes you don't want to insert. Instead, you want the new words to type right on top of the words already on a QBASIC line.

You can type over words if you want—but first you'll have to press the Insert key. Then whatever you type goes right on top of what was there—and takes its place. QBASIC always lets you insert words, unless you press the Insert key. Press it once to stop inserting; press it again to let you insert again.

What If You Want to Add a Line?

You'll notice that program lines in this book are numbered. That's because "regular" BASIC requires you to number each line of instruction so the computer will know when to follow it—but QBASIC users don't have to number lines. You'll also notice in this book that some lines are numbered by tens. That's a trick programmers use to allow themselves room for extra lines, in case they want to add more instructions later.

You can add a line of instructions in a QBASIC program. Just put the cursor where you want to add a line. Then start typing the new line. If you are inserting, your line will fit in and scoot everything over. Press Enter at the end of your new line.

QBASIC Users!

Line numbers are optional in QBASIC—you can use them if you want, but you really don't need them at all.

What If You Want to Take Out a Line?

It's easy to erase words you don't want. Use the arrow keys to place the cursor over the letters you don't want—and then press the Delete key to erase each letter you don't need.

If you want to take a line out of your QBASIC program, just place the cursor at the beginning of the line. Then press the Delete key to erase each letter in the line. Or, to be different, put the cursor at the end of the line and use the Backspace key. The Backspace key backs up the cursor to the left and wipes out everything as it goes.

A Bit of Advice for All Users

Here's some advice for *all* users of BASIC no matter what version you use. If you're already good at typing on a computer keyboard, you'll find it easy to give your computer BASIC programs and commands. You'll be doing *lots* of typing with BASIC.

You'll also be using the number keys often—as well as the parentheses ( ). Those are kind of hard to type at first, but after awhile you'll be so fast at keyboarding you won't believe it. You'll also find you're making fewer mistakes. The more you practice at it, the easier it gets.

If your BASIC programs don't work the way you think they should, always look for one of these problems:

1. Is there an incorrect *line number* somewhere in the program? (QBASIC users—you don't have to worry about line numbers unless you want to.)

2. Did you spell something wrong? Check all the words in your program (carefully).

3. Did you use the wrong punctuation—such as commas, parentheses, quotation marks, or single quotes?

If you still can't figure out the problem, try not to get too worried or angry. Take a break from the keyboard for awhile, and remember: it's OK to ask for help!

To Make a Long Story Short . . .

This chapter told you about what BASIC is and how to start it. We looked at how to enter, run, and change a program in both versions.

QBASIC users can use help screens when they have a question. The pull-down menus make choosing a new command easy.

BASIC, BASICA and GWBASIC users must type in all the commands, since those versions do not have pull-down menus. If you own one of these older versions, you will need a good book to help you with programming questions, since there aren't any help screens. But with this book as your guide, you can learn to write fun programs. Go on to the next chapter to find out more.

CHAPTER THREE

PROGRAMMING THE ADVENTURE

You are skateboarding along your favorite section of sidewalk when you hear a gooey, drippy slime monster at your side. Think fast! Should you face the mutant, continue skateboarding on the path, or run away?

D on't panic. This is just part of an adventure game you can learn how to program in BASIC programming language.

The best way to learn BASIC is to study examples. (See the examples in Appendix D.) Let's see what an adventure program like this might look like.

Running a Program from the Disk

O n the disk that came with this book, there is a program called SLIME.BAS. This is just a short program example—it doesn't have graphics, color, or sound. You'll learn how to add these things later. The next two sections will show you how to run this program, depending on what version of BASIC you have.

For "Regular" BASIC Users Only

1. Put the program disk in the A: floppy drive. (If you have copied the programs to a hard drive, skip this step.)

2. Press the F3 key. This will put the word LOAD on your screen.

3. Type A:SLIME and then press the Enter key. This loads the program from the disk and puts it in the computer's memory. (If you have copied the programs to a hard drive, type C:\BWB\SLIME. The \ is different from a regular /.)

4. To run the program, press the F2 key.

For QBASIC Users Only

1. Put the program disk in the A: floppy drive. (If you have copied the programs to a hard drive, skip this step.)

2. Hold down the Alt key and press F. This "pulls down" the File menu at the top of your screen.

3. Use your arrow keys to highlight the word Open. Then press the Enter key.

4. A large box will appear on your screen. Type A:SLIME.BAS and press Enter. (If you have copied the programs to a hard drive, type C:\BWB\SLIME.BAS. The \ is different from a regular /.)

5. While holding down the Shift key, press F5. This will run the program.

```
You are skateboarding along your favorite section of sidewalk
when you hear a gooey, drippy slime monster at your side.

Think fast!

DO YOU
(1) CHOOSE TO TURN AND FACE THE MUTANT?
(2) CONTINUE ON YOUR RIDE?
(3) RUN AWAY?
TYPE IN YOUR CHOICE AND PRESS ENTER
?
```

This is part of the SLIME.BAS program.

What Do You Think?

Did you successfully run the SLIME.BAS program? (Look at the picture of the computer
screen.) Now you should have a good idea of how adventure games work. Let's talk about
how you can get started creating your own adventure game.

You'll Get Lost Without a Map

Before you make a computer program, you'll need to make up a good adventure story.
You can look in Appendix C, at the back of this book, for some ideas on how to put
together a good story.

The adventure story is the application for this computer program. As we learned in
Chapter 1, we have to understand the application well before we can begin to write the
computer program for it.

One way to understand the adventure is to map out the story. This map of the slime
monster adventure—like a road map you would take along on a vacation trip in your car—
lets you see how the story parts fit together.

Would you go on a road trip to a faraway city without a map? What would happen? After you get far enough away from home, you wouldn't know any of the streets. Every time you turned onto a new road, you'd get lost.

Finally you'd forget what direction you should go. You might get too frustrated to go on—then quit and find your way back home. If only you had taken a map along to help you figure out where and when to turn, and which roads to take!

Maps Are for Programs, Too

You need maps in computer programming too. It really helps to make a picture of your application. Use a pencil—with a good eraser so you can make changes. Getting a picture down on paper will help you later on, when you put the story game into a computer program.

Computer programs often get long and confusing. The drawing will keep you from getting lost, frustrated, and ready to quit!

Our drawing uses boxes to show a group of instructions, or some kind of computer activity. You begin the drawing at the top, and wind your way down through the lines (which are like paths). If you want to find new ways to solve a problem or plan an activity, try drawing a map of it—making a picture can help.

When you make a map or drawing of the whole problem, you should use the same symbols that computer programmers use—like these:

⬚ A box shows an activity.   ◇ A diamond shows a decision.

⟶ Lines and arrows show the order of the steps the program must take.

Let's look at the map of the slime monster adventure. See if you can follow the steps of the program. Does the map seem to go with the story at the beginning of this chapter?

Now that we have a map of the slime monster story, let's think about how we want the computer screen to look during the game.

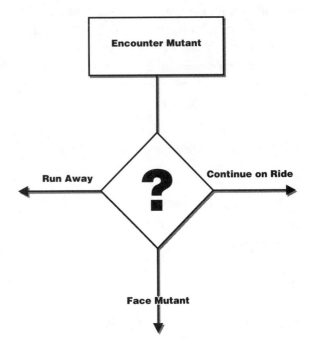

- ■ We want the story to print out on the screen for the player to read.

- ■ Next the computer will ask the player how he wants to answer the question.

- ■ Then the game will jump to the different part of the story, depending on the player's answer.

It's pretty simple. The player reads, answers a question, then the program goes on to a new part of the story.

Try This!

Try to make a map of something you do every day—like making breakfast! Try it. See if you can list all the steps and get everything in the right order. Don't forget: boxes show the activity, diamonds show a decision.

Learn Some BASIC Program Commands

Here is a **program listing** (a list of the instruction lines) from the slime monster program for you to look at.

We will study this section so you can get an idea of what a BASIC program looks like. Don't try to type it in. It won't work by itself. This is just a small section of a larger program. (The entire program is on the floppy disk that came with this book.)

```
10   CLS
20   PRINT "You are skateboarding along your favorite section of sidewalk"
30   PRINT "when you hear a gooey, drippy slime monster at your side."
40   PRINT
50   PRINT "Think fast!"
60   REM The following section shows player the possible choices
70   PRINT
80   PRINT "DO YOU"
90   PRINT "(1) CHOOSE TO TURN AND FACE THE MUTANT? "
100  PRINT "(2) CONTINUE ON YOUR RIDE?"
110  PRINT "(3) RUN AWAY?"
120  PRINT "TYPE IN YOUR CHOICE AND PRESS ENTER"
130  INPUT CHOICE
```

This section of the program tells the computer to do several things:

1. Erase the computer screen. (CLS)

2. Print the story about hearing the slime monster. (PRINT)

3. Print the choices the player gets to make. (PRINT)

4. Ask the player to enter a choice 1, 2, or 3. (INPUT)

It's that simple—but it takes detailed instructions to get the computer to do these tasks.

We'll go over these lines of commands and what they do. First let's talk about lines.

Line Numbers

The computer reads a BASIC program in **line number order**, from smallest to largest. The computer also reads each line from left to right, which is in the same order that you read a page in a book.

TechnoBabble

The BASIC program keeps all the lines of a program in **line number order**. Each line has a special number at the beginning. BASIC sorts them, and keeps them in the right order.

A **line number** can be any number between 0 and 65,529. (BASIC won't let you go over 65,529 lines!) Do you see that the line numbers in the slime monster listing are counted by tens? They could be numbered by ones—or hundreds for that matter. Most programmers number the lines by tens or hundreds. That's so that they can go back later and add more instructions in between those that are already there.

Notice that each new line in our slime monster example starts with a line number. The computer will always follow the number order. For example, if you typed in line number 100 before line number 30, the computer would still read line 30 first. (Because 30 comes before 100!)

What Do the Words in the Program Mean?

Sometimes the command is easy to understand because it looks like a word in English that you already understand. Let's look at some commands you'll be using.

PRINT

Look at line number 20 from our slime monster example:

```
20 PRINT "You are skateboarding along your favorite section of
    sidewalk"
```

20 is the line number, followed by a space, and then the BASIC command PRINT. The words inside quotation marks (" ") tell the computer what message to put on the computer screen.

Look at line number 70:

```
70 PRINT
```

This statement just prints a blank line. There is no message typed here to print. You can use blank lines like this in your programs to make the screen easier to read, or nicer to look at.

Tip Offs

The quotation marks in a PRINT command do not print out on the computer screen when you run the program.

CLS

Look at line number 10 from the program listing:

```
10 CLS
```

This line tells the computer to clear the computer screen. CLS is short for **CL**ear **S**creen. (You learned about this in Chapter 2.)

TechnoBabble

The **PRINT** command tells the computer to put whatever you've typed onto the computer screen. But the things you want shown on the screen must be inside quotation marks "Like this."

REM

Look at line number 60:

```
60  REM The following section shows player the possible choices
```

This line adds a **remark**, or message, to the program listing. REM is short for **REM**ark. A remark doesn't really *do* anything as far as the computer is concerned. It's like making a note to yourself to remind you what's going on in your program.

REM statements are good because they make listings easier to understand for people who look at them later. Long programs can get very confusing. Remarks placed throughout the program help the programmer understand what is going on in that section.

There's another way to add notes to a program listing. A single quotation mark (') starts a comment on any line.

Tip Offs

Here are some examples of remark statements you could place at the beginning of a program:

```
1 REM The name of this program is SLIME.BAS
2 REM Johnny Smith created this fantastic game program
3 REM The slime monster comes at you, and you must
4 REM decide what to do. You get 3 choices, and then
5 REM funny things happen.
```

TechnoBabble

The **CLS** command clears your screen.

The **REM** command lets you add notes to your program so that you can remember what's going on.

The **INPUT** command tells the computer to wait for someone to type in information and press Enter. You use this command when your program asks a question and has to wait until someone answers before it can continue.

A **variable** is a programming instruction that stores information. That information can be answers to questions that the program asks. A variable can be numbers or letters.

INPUT

Look at line number 130 from the slime monster program list:

```
130 INPUT CHOICE
```

The **INPUT** command tells the computer to wait until someone types something on the keyboard and then presses the Enter key.

The computer will wait—forever, if it has to—until the person at the keyboard presses the Enter key. In our adventure game, that person is the player. You use this command when you want your program to ask a question and wait for an answer before continuing. You will get a chance to try out the word INPUT in a little bit.

Variables

Look at line number 130 again:

```
130 INPUT CHOICE
```

The word CHOICE is a **variable**. Programs use variables to hold pieces of information. That information could be numbers, names, letters, or messages. The information can change throughout the program, but the name of the variable will stay the same. (You can give your variable any name—it doesn't have to be CHOICE.)

Think of a variable as a storage box. It's like a little container in the computer that holds information until the program needs it.

Here, our variable called CHOICE could hold just about anything the person at the keyboard types in—such as *Hello* or *Christy Smith* or *3* or *stegosaurus*. You don't know ahead of time what the variable called CHOICE will hold. You have to wait until a player decides what key to press. That's why it's so much fun to use variables in your adventures. Players can make a different choice each time they play the game.

Let's say the player presses 3. Then the variable, CHOICE, would contain the number 3. In other words, CHOICE *equals* 3.

You could even do arithmetic with variables. If you tell the computer to print your name CHOICE number of times, can you guess how many times it would be done? (If you said 3 times, you're right.)

Variables can be used with many other BASIC commands besides INPUT. Try the next activity using the PRINT command you just learned about.

Here is a small program that lets you play around with a variable named WISH. Type this:

```
1 CLS
2 PRINT "Enter a number between 1 and 1000"
3 INPUT WISH
4 PRINT "I wish I had "; WISH; " dollars!"
```

Now run this program. (Regular BASIC users press the F2 key. QBASIC users hold the Shift key and press F5.) When you see the ? on your screen, type in a number (between 1 and 1000) and press the Enter key. Each time you run this program, you could enter a different number, and the variable called WISH would hold that number.

Is the Variable a Number or a Letter?

Here's an important thing to know about variables. The computer needs to know if the variable contains numbers or combinations of letters and numbers.

What's the difference? Who cares? Maybe you don't, but the computer does.

Look at line number 130 again:

```
130 INPUT CHOICE
```

If a variable is **numeric**, then it holds numbers only. (Numeric means numbers.) A numeric variable cannot hold any letter from the alphabet. If you tried to put a letter in it, you would get an error message because the computer expects a number. You can use a numeric variable to do math calculations.

If your variable is **alphanumeric** (which means letters and numbers), then it can hold letters or combinations of letters and numbers (such as names and addresses). Alphanumeric variables must always have a dollar sign at the end of their names, for example:

```
CHOICE$   or   ANSWER$
```

But what would happen if you tried to use an alphanumeric variable to do a math calculation? Your program would get an error message. Alphanumeric variables can never work in a math calculation. The computer won't treat them like numbers, even if they happen to hold a number. To tell an alphanumeric variable apart from a numeric one, look for the dollar sign. Here are some examples:

Alphanumeric	Numeric
CHOICE$ = "A"	CHOICE = 1
CHOICE$ = "2"	NUMBER = 5
NUMBER$ = "5"	
NUMBER$ = "FIVE"	

Variables are very important to any BASIC program. Some BASIC commands use information from variables to add action and suspense to adventure games.

How to Let the Player Make Choices

Adventure games are interesting because the player gets to make decisions and then see what happens next. Depending on the player's decision, the story can go in more than one direction.

Some decisions are as simple as whether or not to play the game again (all that one takes is a quick YES or NO answer). Some decisions let the player pick one of several choices for the next plot. (Any decision the player makes will cause the computer to go to a special part of the program. The next section will tell you how BASIC does this.)

Here is a listing of another section of the slime monster program. Try to figure out what this section is supposed to do.

```
130 INPUT CHOICE
140 IF CHOICE = 2 THEN GOTO 210
150 IF CHOICE = 3 THEN GOTO 260
160 IF CHOICE <> 1 THEN GOTO 60
170 REM CHOICE1: FACE MUTANT
```

Line 140 tells the computer that if the player picks 2, the program should "jump" to line number 210. If the player picks 3, the program jumps to line number 260.

Line 160 uses the "not equal to" symbol, <>. This line tells the computer that if the player picks any number that isn't equal to 1, the program should jump back to line number 60. Line 60 is a remark that starts the question over again. If the player picks 1, the next line number will be 170.

Do you understand this section of the program? There are two new important BASIC commands going on here. They are:

- IF and THEN

- GOTO

Keep reading to learn how these work.

Decisions, Decisions!

This BASIC command uses two words which you probably use every day when you talk to your friends. For example:

> "*If* you give me a piece of your candy, *then* I will give you half of my sandwich."

> "*If* you pick up your room, *then* I will let you play Nintendo."

> "*If* you have $6.75, *then* you can go to the movie."

BASIC uses these words in much the same way you do. Look at line number 140:

```
140 IF CHOICE = 2 THEN GOTO 210
```

Line number 140 tells the computer that *if* number 2 was the player's choice, *then* the program will jump ahead to line 210. If the player's choice was *not* the number 2, then the computer simply goes to the next line after line 140.

Comparing Numbers

Computers are very good at comparing numbers. You have been comparing numbers since you were in first grade. Remember these?

<	is less than
>	is greater than
<>	is not equal to
=	is equal to

You probably remember tests you took in grade school where you had to put the correct sign between two numbers. It's pretty easy, but you probably will make mistakes if you start to get tired of looking at a page full of numbers.

Guess what? Computers never make mistakes when it comes to comparing numbers. Computers never get bored— or tired—the way people can. That's why computers are so useful for comparing those dull, boring numbers, over and over again.

Look at line number 160:

```
160 IF CHOICE <> 1 THEN GOTO 60
```

- If CHOICE contains any number other than 1, the next instruction would be on line number 60.

- If CHOICE does equal 1, the computer can find the next instruction on the next line after 160.

Take Off with GOTO

The BASIC command GOTO works just like the words "go to." For example:

> "Let's go to the Mall!"

> "I want to go to the library."

> "I will go to baseball practice at 1:00."

GOTO simply tells the computer to jump to a line number in a different part of the program. This is called **branching** in the program.

GOTO is used with IF and THEN in the following line (number 150 from the slime monster program):

```
150 IF N = 3 THEN GOTO 260
```

Line number 150 tells the computer to jump to line number 260—but only if CHOICE holds the number 3.

Tip Offs

Those < and > symbols are on the keyboard on the bottom row. Just hold down the Shift key when you type the , (comma) or . (period).

TechnoBabble

Programmers call the GOTO command **branching**. To understand computer branching, think of a tree. A tree starts from the ground as a trunk. As it gets taller, the limbs branch out in every direction. A computer program follows directions that way. When the program starts out, the computer does each of its instructions in order. But when the program comes to a GOTO instruction—or several of them in a row—then the program branches out to follow them, like the branches of a tree.

An **END** statement tells the computer program to stop. This is usually used on the last line of the program.

You can use GOTO by itself, without the IF and THEN command. For instance, what if the computer comes to a line like this one?

```
350 GOTO 400
```

What do you think will happen next? What would happen to any lines numbered 360 or 370? (Well—nothing! The computer would skip—that is, branch—to line 400.)

END

The last command to learn in this chapter is the END command. The END statement tells the program to stop—completely. Programmers usually put an END statement on the last line of the program. Here's what one looks like:

```
320 END
```

Without END statements, the program would keep going and going and going.

Make the Program "User-Friendly"

A user-friendly adventure game program is one that has clear instructions. The messages that print on the computer screen should tell what the choices are.

The instructions should tell the player what keys on the keyboard to press. The instructions need to remind the player to press Enter to go on. For instance, look at this section of the slime monster program:

```
 80 PRINT "DO YOU"
 90 PRINT "(1)CHOOSE TO TURN AND FACE THE MUTANT?"
100 PRINT "(2)CONTINUE ON YOUR RIDE?"
110 PRINT "(3)RUN AWAY?"
120 PRINT "TYPE IN YOUR CHOICE AND PRESS ENTER"
130 INPUT CHOICE
140 IF CHOICE = 2 THEN GOTO 210
150 IF CHOICE = 3 THEN GOTO 260
160 IF CHOICE <> 1 THEN GOTO 60
```

Humans Make Mistakes

Some things can mess up a computer program. Sometimes the player can make a mistake while typing in the choice. But you can design programs which avoid some of these problems. You figure out the kinds of mistakes that might happen. Then you plan instructions to take care of those mistakes, so they don't mess up the game.

In the slime monster game, what happens if the player presses a key which is not a 1, 2, or 3? For instance, what if the player is a bit confused, and makes one of these mistakes:

- Pressing the Enter key without making a choice?

- Pressing some number key (like 8 or 4)?

- Pressing a letter key such as E? (This could happen, since E is right next to the 3 on the keyboard.)

This program checks for those errors by using these statements:

```
130 INPUT CHOICE
140 IF CHOICE = 2 THEN GOTO 210
150 IF CHOICE = 3 THEN GOTO 260
160 IF CHOICE <> 1 THEN GOTO 60
```

If the player types anything but 1, 2, or 3, the statements keep the program from continuing. (You'll learn more about catching errors like these when you read the next chapter.)

To Make a Long Story Short . . .

Computer adventure games are a good example of what BASIC can do. Adventures need decisions—and BASIC is good at giving the player lots of choices.

Once the player makes a decision in the game, BASIC makes it simple (with the IF and THEN command) to go to the right place in the adventure. The player can choose from several choices, and BASIC will know how to handle each choice. If the player makes a mistake, BASIC can catch it and handle it, so that it isn't a problem.

The next chapter will show you how to make your program work even better.

CHAPTER FOUR

Slick Tricks

You are one of the last few living red salmon. You are trying to survive the dangers of your long ocean trip back to the river where you were born. You must return there so that you can mate and produce a new generation of red salmon . . . .

You can just barely make out the sunlight streaming through the blue-green ocean above. Suddenly, you see a yellow submarine research station, where scientists are studying this world beneath the waves.

Watch out! A net brushes by your right fin. It could be fishermen, ready to put you into a can for the grocery store. Up ahead is a human in scuba gear. Are they dangerous?

This ocean adventure puts the player in the body of a red salmon, trying to stay alive until it gets back to the place where it hatched. To see what this adventure game looks like on your computer, run the program called OCEAN.BAS. If you're not sure how to do this, see the instructions at the beginning of Chapter 3. Just substitute OCEAN.BAS for SLIME.BAS.

It takes a lot of work to create games. Before anyone can play a game, the programmer has to make sure that everything works smoothly. If there are any errors in the program, they could mess up the whole game. They might even cause the program to stop. The programmer also has to think of mistakes the player might make while playing the game. Those kinds of mistakes can really mess up a program too.

In this chapter, you'll learn how to fix mistakes and make your programs run better. You'll also get some tips on how to make a program game easy to play. And you'll find out how to make an adventure game more interesting.

Watch Out for Bugs!

Programmers have a special name for any kind of error that makes a computer program mess up. It's called a **bug**.

Because they're people, programmers can make mistakes while setting up a program. Part of their job is to catch those errors. It's a little like trapping a real bug—keeping that bug from getting loose and messing up the program. When they set out to catch their own mistakes, programmers actually call it **error trapping**.

To fix your own programming bugs, you need to practice running your program over and over again. Make sure every instruction works like it's supposed to. Look for problems like these:

- incorrect line numbers
- incorrect spelling
- wrong punctuation

Once you've figured out your own bugs, then you have to worry about mistakes the player might make.

TechnoBabble

A **bug** is an error in a program that keeps it from working right. Programmers try to catch their own mistakes by **error trapping**. Another kind of bug is a mistake a user might make—and it's up to the programmer to catch that mistake before it's made!

Players Make Mistakes, Too!

The people who play your computer game will probably make mistakes and errors. Some errors make your program stop. Other errors make the game come out all wrong. But you can fix up your program to prevent most errors.

As a computer programmer, one of your jobs—once you've caught your own little bugs—is to figure out what kinds of mistakes the *players* might make. Once you've done that, you can set some different traps in your program—to keep the game going smoothly, even if the player makes a mistake.

How do you prevent or fix player mistakes? Read the next few sections to find out about some common player mistakes, and how to prevent or trap those errors. You'll find examples from several of the programs that came with this book.

Problem: What Do I Do Now?

If players don't know which key to press, what do they do? They might press the Esc key, if they think that might allow them to quit your game. They might press one of the function keys, if they think those are help keys, like in other games or programs they use. How do players know whether the choices are A, B, or C (or 1, 2, or 3)? Or whether to type a capital Y or a lowercase y for Yes? When players get frustrated, they start typing any old key, hoping that something will work.

Solution: Make the Choices Very Clear

You can print the choices and instructions on the screen to help the player know what to do next. Here is a sample of this from the OCEAN.BAS program you just ran. Don't try to type these lines into your computer. Just look at them and see if you can understand what they do.

```
6210    PRINT "DO YOU:"
6220    PRINT "1) Stay put so the scuba diver doesn't see you?"
```

```
6230  PRINT "2) Turn around and swim like crazy?"
6250  PRINT "Type in your choice and press ENTER"
```

Now the player will know to type a 1 or 2, and then press Enter. The programmer made it very clear.

Problem: Oops, I Pressed the Wrong Number!

The player's finger might slip and press 5 by accident, even though you have told him to press 1, 2, or 3, or yes or no.

Solution: Bad Choices Not Allowed!

Your program can let the player enter certain keys *only*. Look at this section from a program.

```
130 INPUT CHOICE
140 IF Choice = 2 THEN GOTO 210
150 IF Choice = 3 THEN GOTO 260
160 IF Choice <> 1 THEN GOTO 60
```

If the player types 1, 2, or 3, the computer goes on to the correct line. If the choice is not a 1, 2, or 3, the computer goes back to line 60, which is the line that prints the question again.

Problem: The Player Forgets to Press the Enter Key!

Players might press the correct number but forget to press the Enter key. A player might sit there all day, and wait for something to happen. He or she would think your game doesn't work very well. Your game works just fine, but you need to tell the player how to play it!

Solution: Don't Just Sit There, Do Something!

Look at the line below.

```
120 PRINT "Type in your choice and press ENTER"
```

Line 120 prints a message on the screen to remind players to type their choice *and then* press the Enter key.

Problem: Should the Answer Be *Y* or *y*?

What if your game tells players to press Y for *yes* and N for *no*. A player might press lowercase y or n. That's okay with you, but the computer still doesn't think the lowercase letters are the same as uppercase choices.

Solution: By Any Other Name, It's Still a *Y*

These sample program lines show how a program can use *Y, y, N,* or *n.*

```
0350 REM Don't let the player enter anything but Y,y,N,n
0360 IF YesNo$ = "y" OR YesNo$ = "Y" THEN GOTO 440
0370 IF YesNo$ = "n" OR YesNo$ = "N" THEN GOTO 390
0380 GOTO 0330
0390 END
```

Lines 0360 and 0370 use the IF and THEN commands. Look at the word OR in line 0360. This line means "If the choice is *Y* or *y,* go to line 0440." Line 0370 sends the computer to line 390 if *n* or *N* is the choice. Line 0380 tells the computer to ask the question all over again at Line 0330 if a player chooses any letter besides *N.*

Well, now you know of some ways to prevent player mistakes. Would you like to learn how to make a game program more interesting to play? Read on . . . .

Surprise, Surprise!

Some games you might have on your computer seem different every time you play. How do they do that? It's all in the planning and programming instructions.

For example, let's say you're programming an adventure game that has six different adventures the player can try. You want the computer to give the player a different game to play each time. First, you've got to plan out what the six adventures will be (remember when we talked about mapping out your program in Chapter 3?). Then, you've got to write these six different adventures into your program. This next program example from the OCEAN.BAS game will show you how the computer can go into six different adventures.

```
300 REM Computer picks next adventure
310 ADVENTURE = INT(6*RND(1)) + 1
320 IF ADVENTURE = 1 THEN GOTO 1000
330 IF ADVENTURE = 2 THEN GOTO 2000
340 IF ADVENTURE = 3 THEN GOTO 3000
350 IF ADVENTURE = 4 THEN GOTO 4000
360 IF ADVENTURE = 5 THEN GOTO 5000
370 IF ADVENTURE = 6 THEN GOTO 6000
```

Line 310 mixes up the six adventures and picks a new one each time.

How does it do that? Line 310 has a math formula that lets the computer pick a number between 1 and 6. The **variable**, ADVENTURE, holds that number. In Chapter 6, you'll learn more about how the computer can pick an unpredictable number.

Do you see all those IF statements in lines 320 through 370? Based on which number the computer picks, those IF commands send the player to the section where each adventure begins.

Giving a game different actions to follow isn't so hard after all. But what about those times you want your program to do the same action over and over again? Read this next section to find out how.

Here We Go Loop-de-Loop

Bobby: Pete and Repeat sat on a fence. Pete fell off and who was left?

Kevin: Repeat.

Bobby: Okay. Pete and Repeat sat on a fence. Pete fell off and who was left?

Kevin: Repeat.

Bobby: Okay. Pete and Repeat sat on a fence. Pete fell off and who was left?

Kevin: Repeat.

Okay, you get the idea. This joke never ends. The riddle repeats over and over.

TechnoBabble

Sometimes a program has to repeat the same steps over and over again. This is called a **loop**.

Computers are great at doing things over and over again, just like this crazy riddle. There are many times when your program will repeat some little activity over and over—like counting a list of things. When a computer needs to repeat part of a program over and over, it is called a **loop**. A person would probably repeat the riddle two or three times, and then chuckle and quit. A computer will repeat a loop forever unless you tell it to stop. Computers never get bored like people do.

You should learn how to repeat lines a certain number of times in any program. There is a pair of BASIC commands that lets you repeat computer lines over and over until you want them to stop. This pair works together as a team. It is called a **FOR...NEXT** loop.

The FOR command tells the computer how many times to repeat the loop. It goes at the beginning of the loop.

TechnoBabble

The **FOR** and **NEXT** commands allow you to repeat an activity. FOR tells how many times to repeat; NEXT keeps track of how many times the activity repeats.

NEXT does two jobs. It adds 1 to the variable that keeps track of how many times to do the loop. That's like saying, "We'll do it one more time!" NEXT also sends the computer back to the FOR, so the loop can start over again.

A loop can be very helpful in many computer programs.

Try This!

Let's program the riddle!

The riddle would never end unless you tell the computer to repeat it only a few times. That's why the loop only repeats three times. This program is on your disk. You can load and run it, or try typing it in yourself.

```
10   REM Program Pete.BAS Program to repeat riddle
20   CLS
30   PRINT "Bobby: Hey, Kevin! Try to guess the right answer!"
40   FOR COUNT = 1 TO 3
50   PRINT "Bobby: Pete and Repeat sat on a fence."
60   PRINT "    Pete fell off and who was left?"
70   PRINT "Kevin: Repeat?"
80   PRINT "Bobby: OK,"
85   PRINT
90   NEXT COUNT
100  PRINT "Kevin: I get it, now. Very funny!"
110  PRINT "    Let's get some ice cream now!
120  END
```

The loop includes lines 40–90. That's the part that repeats. Line 40 says, starting with 1, do these lines until we get to 3. Then the message prints.

Line 90 does two things. First it adds 1 to the COUNT variable. It also sends the program back to the FOR in line 40 to do it all again.

Here's another fun way to see how easily a loop can handle a lot of repeats. You can try this program to print an important message on the screen 10 times.

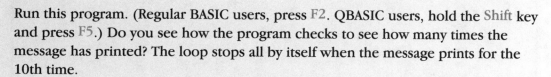

Try This!

Type this program. It prints *Pizza Party!!!* 10 times.

```
NEW
10 FOR COUNT = 1 TO 10
20    PRINT COUNT," Pizza Party!!!"
30 NEXT COUNT
40 END
```

Run this program. (Regular BASIC users, press F2. QBASIC users, hold the Shift key and press F5.) Do you see how the program checks to see how many times the message has printed? The loop stops all by itself when the message prints for the 10th time.

QBASIC Users!

You can also use DO...LOOP commands to repeat computer tasks. Here's an example of how it's used—a program that is the same as that in the activity.

```
DO UNTIL COUNT = 11
    PRINT COUNT, " Pizza
    Party!!!"
    COUNT = COUNT + 1
LOOP
```

Another important trick to make a program fun is to make it look nice on the screen. This next section shows you how.

Lookin' Good!

Sometimes your adventure needs quite a few words to explain the plot. But if there are too many words, the screen can start to look too confusing. If players get *bored* (that nasty "b"-word), they'll turn off the game.

After all, you don't want your players to think they're just reading a book instead of playing a game. Players don't want to read too much at one time. Take a look at this wordy screen:

```
You are a one of the last few
living red salmon.
You are trying to survive the dangers of your long
ocean trek back to the river where you were born.
You must return there so you can mate and
produce a new generation of red salmon.
Along your journey there are many dangers.   Can
your species survive another generation?
To start your next adventure,
press any key    (or Q to quit)
```

Do you think you would like to read this boring screen?

Give Me Some Space!

If your game has a wordy description like the example above, there are some ways to keep your player's interest.

There is an easy way to make the screens easier to look at and read. You can just add some PRINT statements to space out paragraphs. You should pick natural breaks in the sentences.

Study this part of the OCEAN.BAS program on your disk. Notice there are some extra statements. These add blank lines to the screen.

```
30 PRINT "You are a one of the last few living red salmon."
40 PRINT
45 PRINT
50 PRINT "You are trying to survive the dangers of your long"
60 PRINT "ocean trek back to the river where you were born."
70 PRINT "You must return there so you can mate and "
80 PRINT "produce a new generation of red salmon."
90 PRINT
```

```
100 PRINT
110 PRINT "Along your journey there are many dangers. Can"
120 PRINT "your species survive another generation?"
130 PRINT
140 PRINT
150 PRINT
160 PRINT
170 PRINT
180 PRINT "To start your next adventure,"
190 PRINT "press any key, (or Q to quit)"
```

Here's what the screen will look like. Doesn't this screen look nicer and easier to read?

```
You are one of the last few living red salmon.

You are trying to survive the dangers of your long
ocean trek back to the river where you were born.
You must return there so you can mate and
produce a new generation of red salmon.

Along your journey there are many dangers.  Can
your species survive another generation?




To start your next adventure,
press any key  (or Q to quit)
```

This screen is easier to read, don't you agree?

Read at Your Own Speed

Here is another way to break up all that reading. Every player reads at a different speed. Make your program print just a few sentences on the screen at one time. Let the player choose when to read more. Here's how one part in the ocean program lets players read at their own pace.

```
6500 REM CHOICE2:
6505  CLS
6510  PRINT "As you turn around, your tail gets caught"
6520  PRINT "in the net. You struggle to free yourself, but"
6530  PRINT "you feel yourself being pulled through the water."
6540  PRINT
6550  PRINT "(Press any key to continue)"
6560   WHILE INKEY$ = "": WEND
6570  PRINT
6580  PRINT "To make matters worse, here comes the scuba diver,"
6590  PRINT "carrying a knife. Oh no, it looks like this is it"
6600  PRINT "for you.
6610  PRINT
6620  PRINT "(Press any key to continue)"
6630   WHILE INKEY$ = "": WEND
```

Line 6550 is a simple print statement that tells your player to press any key to continue. The next line is the trick.

```
6560 WHILE INKEY$ = "": WEND
```

Line 6560 uses **INKEY$** to let a player press any key. As soon as a player presses any key, the computer goes on to the next line.

INKEY$ is a new BASIC word for you to learn. INKEY$ is sort of like INPUT$ because the computer waits for the player to type something on the keyboard. But, INKEY$ does not need the player to press the Enter key to go on, like INPUT$ does.

INKEY$ is really just a variable that holds only one character. INKEY$ can be empty, or can hold any character. INKEY$ starts out holding nothing; it's just blank. When a player presses any key, INKEY$ then equals that key. So line 6560 says "While INKEY$ is empty, I'll wait. But as soon as the player presses a key, I'll go on."

TechnoBabble

The **INKEY$** command works like the INPUT$ command. (Remember, the INPUT command tells the computer to wait for an answer before continuing.) The INKEY$ command waits for any old button to be pressed.

To Make a Long Story Short . . .

You learned how to:

- Avoid player mistakes.
- Create surprise plot twists.
- Create loops in the program to repeat routines over and over.
- Make your screens easier to read.

CHAPTER FIVE

WHO'S THE BOSS?

Okay, campers, here is what we have to do today! Jessica, you go get the wood for the fire. Eric, unload the cooking gear. Abbie, you need to get some water. When you get back, unpack the fishing gear. Sam, you and Bill put up the tent. Now get busy, everybody! And don't come back until you're finished! I, your fearless leader, will sit here and guard the food.

It sounds like these kids have a bossy leader. What does that have to do with computer programming? You'll find out that a good computer program has a "boss" to tell the rest of the program how to get the job done. This "boss" keeps the program organized.

This chapter will show you how to make the first section of your program the boss that tells the whole program what to do and when to do it. This will help you get organized.

Turn Big Jobs into Little Jobs

A program does a big job. Even a simple program has many instructions. The best way to build a computer program is to break a big job down into smaller jobs. Smaller jobs are easier to work on. You write the program for each small job. Then you put it all together to do the big job.

It is sort of like when you and your family go out to buy some groceries for your camping trip. Your mom goes to the produce section, your sister heads to the cereal aisle, your brother goes to the milk case, and you head for the candy aisle. (Hey, you can't forget those s'mores!) Everybody has a part to play. Even Dad has a job. He's waiting at the curb with the car running.

Once you get to the campground, you all work on jobs that get your campsite ready. Your sister unloads the sleeping bags, Mom and Dad put up the tent, your brother starts the stove, and you lay out the s'mores. Everybody takes care of a job.

Programs should handle big jobs the way your family does. They break the big job down into smaller jobs.

Who's the Boss?

The beginning of the program is the main part, the boss. The main part lists all the little jobs and tells the computer when to do each little job.

Let's pretend your family's camp-out is a computer program. The main part of your camping program might look like this:

```
10   REM Camp Out
20   MAIN
30      GOSUB 500        'Buy groceries
40      GOSUB 600        'Put gas in car
50      GOSUB 700        'Drive to campground
60      GOSUB 800        'Unload groceries
70      GOSUB 900        'Put up tent
```

Do you see the statement **GOSUB** in this example? That means, "Go do a little job, and don't come back until you are finished." The comments in these lines tell you what those little jobs, or **subroutines**, are.

The next listing is the main part of a real computer program called 8BALLSUB.BAS, which is on your disk. It is not the whole program, only the main part, the boss. Look for the GOSUB commands.

TechnoBabble

The word **GOSUB** is short for "*Go* do a *Sub*routine." Programmers call little jobs subroutines. GOSUB means, "Go do a subroutine. Come back when you finish."

```
100 REM Program 8BALLSUB.BAS  'Structured Program
200 REM Simulates an 8-Ball toy
300 GOSUB 1300    'Housekeeping:
400 GOSUB 4200  'Play or not:
500 IF YESNO$ = "N" THEN GOTO 800
600 GOSUB 5400    'Shake 8 Ball:
700 GOTO 400    'Find out if player wants to play again
800 REM Player doesn't want to play anymore
900 CLS
1000 PRINT "Wasn't that fun?"
1100 PRINT "See you later"
1200 END
```

Organize Those Little Jobs

The main part of the program appears at the beginning of the program listing. The subroutines, or little jobs, appear near the end of the program. And why is that? If the main part is first, you can look at any program and tell almost right away what that program is all about.

The little jobs—subroutines—do all the work. The line numbers still have to be in order, from small to large. Here is a sample of a subroutine from the 8BALLSUB.BAS program. This subroutine has one little job: find out if the player wants to play again.

```
4200 REM Play or not:****************************
4300 REM Asks the player whether (s)he wants to play or not
4400    LOCATE 23
4500    PRINT "Would you like to ask the all-knowing 8 Ball a question?"
4600    PRINT "Type in Y for yes, or N to end game, then press ENTER"
4700    INPUT YESNO$
4800    REM Don't let the player enter anything but Y,y,N,n
4900    PRINT "Your answer is "; YESNO$
```

```
5000      IF YESNO$ = "y" OR YESNO$ = "Y" THEN YESNO$ = "Y"
5100      IF YESNO$ = "n" OR YESNO$ = "N" THEN YESNO$ = "N"
5200      IF YESNO$ <> "Y" AND YESNO$ <> "N" THEN GOTO 4600 'Player error
5300 RETURN
```

A subroutine must end with a **RETURN** statement. That tells the computer to go back to the line right after the GOSUB that sent the computer to that subroutine in the first place.

If you organize each program with a main part and follow that with all the subroutines, your program will be easy to read. When you want to change the program later, it will be easy to figure out where to add parts. Every part of the program will be where you expect it to be.

TechnoBabble

A **RETURN** code tells the computer to go back to the line following the GOSUB command that sent it on the little job.

What Happens If the Program Is Not Organized?

Programmers call messy programs *spaghetti code*. Why? Try to imagine a plate of spaghetti noodles. I'm sure that this will be easy to do!

Can you see even one complete noodle, from end to end? Could you trace a noodle as it winds around all the other noodles? Wouldn't that noodle get all mixed up, so you couldn't tell where one noodle ends and the next noodle begins?

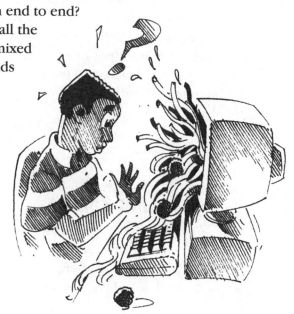

This is what a disorganized computer program starts to seem like—a plate of tangled computer instructions.

How does a program get that way? Probably poor planning. The programmer just sits down to write a program without thinking through the problem. He uses the trial-and-error method ("if at first you don't succeed…"), and plugs away at it until the program is close to what he wants, even if it isn't perfect.

This is why making a map of your program is so important. It puts the ideas on paper. A good programmer can "see" how the information flows through the program.

Even if the trial-and-error-made program works, let's say you later want to modify, change, or improve it. If you make one change, it could mess up the whole program.

Instead, be organized. Break the tasks of the program down into smaller jobs. Do the little jobs in subroutines.

Add More Little Jobs

It is easy to add on more parts to an organized program. For instance, you can add a routine to draw a picture or play music.

These two types of subroutines are really separate programs. The programmer makes them work all by themselves before attaching them to the main part.

When the subroutine program works perfectly on its own, the programmer very carefully adds it to the end of the main program. That is done with the **MERGE** command.

QBASIC Users!

You can skip this next section on using the MERGE command. QBASIC lets you combine subroutines in a different way. Look ahead to the section called "Merging with QBASIC."

TechnoBabble

The **MERGE** command allows you to add programs together, such as subroutines.

The MERGE Command in "Regular" BASIC

There are several steps you should follow when you add a subroutine onto the main program.

First, make sure that both the main program and the subroutine program work perfectly on their own.

The new subroutine should start with a very large line number. That will keep the line numbers in the main programs from getting all mixed up and running into the subroutine.

Here are some specific instructions for you to follow when you have a subroutine to merge.

1 Save the subroutine like this:

```
SAVE"_____.BAS"
```

(You would put the name of your subroutine in the blank.)

2 Load the main program. Here is an example:

```
LOAD"MAINPROG.BAS"
```

(Of course, use the correct name of your main program.)

3 Merge the subroutine program in with the main program by using the MERGE command.

```
MERGE "LITTLE.BAS"
```

Now the two programs are together in one program (with the same name as the main program). The subroutine program is still in your storage area, too, in case you ever need it again for another program.

Once you've added a subroutine to your main program, you'll want to make sure it's "hooked up." For example, you'll need to add a GOSUB line at the beginning of your program that tells your computer to go find your newly merged program. And make sure the subroutine ends with a RETURN line.

Finally, you'll want to test, test, test. Run the whole program several times until you are sure it works okay.

Tip Offs

Every programmer has a "little bag of tricks." That is, a collection of routines. Over time, a programmer makes up routines that do tasks most programs need now and then. Whenever the program needs that type of routine, the programmer just pulls out the subroutine program and adds it to the program. You can make your own "little bag of tricks" as you play around with BASIC.

If you need to make the line numbers larger, don't worry. You can use the **RENUM** command on your main program (or subroutine) and it will redo the line numbers for you.

You don't need to renumber the lines if the subroutine line numbers are already quite large.

Try This!

Type in this little program:

```
10 PRINT "Have a Nice Day"
20 PRINT "Dance until your toes hurt"
30 PRINT "Get Psyched for Fun"
40 END
```

Now, type this command and press the Enter key:

```
RENUM 10000,,100
```

The RENUM command can be used to renumber lines in a program listing. 10000,,100 will start at line number 10000 and number the lines after 100's. The program should now look like this:

```
10000 PRINT "Have a Nice Day"
10100 PRINT "Dance until your toes hurt"
10200 PRINT "Get Psyched for Fun"
10300 END
```

Merging with QBASIC

If you're using QBASIC, you can't use the MERGE command. But that's okay—there's a simple way to include a subroutine in a main program.

You can copy the subroutine and then place it into the main program.

Make sure that both the main program and the subroutine program work perfectly on their own and *save* each one. Test them to make sure each one does what you want it to do. It would be bad to add a subroutine to a large program if the subroutine still has a bug in it.

To merge your subroutine, follow these instructions:

1. Start with your subroutine program. Move the cursor to the top of the program. Hold down the Shift key while you use the arrow key to move to the bottom of the program. That is how you highlight the lines of a program.

2. Now you need to copy the selected, or highlighted, section. Select the Edit menu, highlight the word Copy, and press Enter. Now your subroutine is copied into the **clipboard**—a storage area in the computer memory.

► **3** Next, you should open the main program. Select the File menu, highlight the word New, and press Enter. The screen will ask you if you want to save the program. Answer NO because you have a saved copy on the disk already. Type the name of the main program, or use the Tab key and arrow keys to choose the name from a list of your programs.

► **4** Use the arrow keys to move to the end of the main program. Select the Edit menu, highlight the word Paste and press Enter. That should put the subroutine right at the end of the main program, where you want it!

You'll need to make a few changes to "hook up" your new subroutine. The main part of the program will need a GOSUB to send the computer to the new subroutine at the right time. The subroutine should also include a RETURN statement at the end.

Finally, test, test, test. Run the whole program several times until you are sure it works okay.

An Organized Program Is a Happy Program

Computer programs are complicated enough even when they *are* organized. But organizing sure helps keep things straight when you're working with so many lines and commands.

To Make a Long Story Short . . .

Organized computer programs are easier to make and easier to change than messy programs. Disorganized, messy programs are called *spaghetti code*.

Your programs will be organized if you follow these tips:

■ Break big jobs down into smaller subroutines.

■ Have a main part that uses GOSUB to send the work to subroutines.

Start your own collection of routine programs. You can use these in other programs whenever you need them.

CHAPTER SIX
TRUCKLOADS OF DATA

Gypsies dance and sing in the moonlight. You hear the music of violins and tambourines. A Gypsy woman wearing dangling beads and scarves sits at a table nearby. As you walk up she welcomes you to join in for a look at her Magic 8-Ball. What will it tell you? What mysteries unfold on this night . . . ?

Are you interested in an eerie, mysterious adventure? This story is the beginning to a BASIC computer program that makes your computer act like a Magic 8-Ball. The program is on your disk or hard drive. It's called 8BALLSUB.BAS. Try running this program. (If you're not sure how to run it, see the instructions at the beginning of Chapter 3.)

This program does two things you might want to learn about and use for other programs. First, it shows you how to handle large amounts of information in your program. Second, it shows you how to mix up choices and pick a new one each time. This is handy for programming games of chance like cards or dice.

How Does an 8-Ball Work?

Have you played with a Magic 8-Ball? A Magic 8-Ball looks like a large number-eight pool ball. It is made of plastic and filled with fluid. There is a clear window on the bottom. Little messages float around inside. When you tip it over, one of the many messages floats up to the window, where you can read it.

It's fun to make up questions, shake the Magic 8-Ball, look at the window, and read the message. You can pretend that the message is supposed to be an answer to your question. (Give me a break, right? Of course, it's just for fun.)

Here's the map, or picture, of how the 8-Ball Game works.

When Your Program Needs a Large Amount of Information

This 8-Ball game has 20 different choices for a message, and we need an easy way for the computer to handle them. What do you do when your computer program has a lot of information to keep track of? Take a look at this next example. What if you have to keep track of a bunch of names like this?

Roll Call of Students in Your Classroom

Ashley	Allison
Arthur	Luke
Betsy	Mallory
Steve	

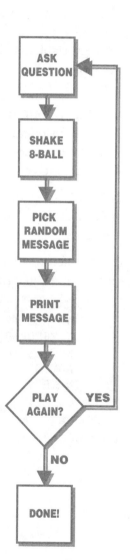

So far you've used a variable to keep track of only one piece of information at a time. (You learned about variables in Chapter 3.)

What happens if you have a whole list of names in your program? You can't have NAME$ = "Ashley" and NAME$ = "Allison" at the same time. How can you keep track of a whole list of names, phone numbers, or collections?

Lists

BASIC has a way to keep track of the lists. You can use a variable that can keep track of whole lists. Each item in the list is part of the variable list. This type of a list is called an **array**.

Each list needs a name, just like a single variable. Use the same rules for naming lists as you use for naming single variables—if the list is made of letters and numbers combined, use $ on the end of the list name.

NAMES$ is a good name for a list variable that holds a name, so we'll use it for our list of students.

TechnoBabble

A computer programmer uses the word **array** whena variable holds a list of information. An array variable name looks just like a regular variable name, except it includes parentheses around a number. Here's an example: **ROLLCALL$(1)**. Each item in the list is called an element. The number inside the parentheses is the element number.

You'll need to keep track of each item in the list NAMES$. You do that with a number in parentheses, like this:

```
NAMES$ (1) = "Ashley"
NAMES$ (2) = "Allison"
NAMES$ (3) = "Arthur"
NAMES$ (4) = "Luke"
NAMES$ (5) = "Mallory"
NAMES$ (6) = "Steve"
```

Each item in the list has its own number. This is a good example for holding names in a class, but what about 20 messages for an 8-ball game? Keep reading.

Setting Up Space for the List

Here's how the 8-Ball program sets up space for the messages. It uses a **DIM** command, which tells the computer the name of the list and how many messages it holds:

```
50 DIM MESSAGE$(20)
```

Before you start adding to a list, the computer has to know how much room to save for holding the list. The computer needs to know—right from the beginning—how much will be in the list.

The 8-Ball game program has an 8-ball with 20 messages in it. The program will put those 20 messages in a list called MESSAGE$. (This program is on your disk. It is named 8BALL.BAS.)

DIM is short for dimension. Dimension means size; for example, the dimension of a box is its size. Choose a number to put in the parentheses that will be big enough to hold the list, but not too big. The DIM statement usually goes at the beginning of a computer program.

For example, a list of your homeroom classmates need a DIM size of 20. A list of your whole school might use a DIM size of 500 to hold all the names in the list. All the names in your town might need a DIM size of 30,000 or 1,000,000.

Load Up the List

Now you have enough room in the computer to hold 20 messages in a list called MESSAGE$. What do you think is in the list? Nothing! The list is empty because you haven't told the computer to put any information in the list yet.

TechnoBabble

The **DIM** command tells the computer the name of your variable list and how much is in it.

If you were making a roll-call list of 20 students in your class, the list would look like this:

Roll-call List

1.

2.

3.

4.

5.

6.

7.

and so on up to 20.

The list is empty right now. If this were a roll call on a piece of paper, it would seem simple enough just to take a pencil and write the names next to the numbers.

BASIC has two commands that take the place of pencil and paper. These two words put the information into the list variable. These words are **DATA** and **READ**. These two words work as a team.

Here are lines 1700 through 3600 from the 8BALLSUB.BAS program:

```
1700 DATA "It is certain"
1800 DATA "Signs point to yes"
1900 DATA "Outlook good"
2000 DATA "My sources say no"
2100 DATA "It is decidedly so"
2200 DATA "You may rely on it"
2300 DATA "Ask again later"
2400 DATA "Better not tell you now"
2500 DATA "Very doubtful"
2600 DATA "Yes, definitely"
2700 DATA "Cannot predict now"
2800 DATA "My reply is no"
2900 DATA "As I see it, yes"
3000 DATA "Don't count on it"
3100 DATA "Outlook not so good"
3200 DATA "Without a doubt"
3300 DATA "Really hazy, try again"
3400 DATA "Concentrate and ask again"
3500 DATA "Yes"
3600 DATA "No"
```

These are the DATA statements. Each line has the DATA command, and then the 8-Ball message in quotation marks. The DATA statements should be together in the program. They can be at the beginning of the program or near the end.

The next step is to put these messages into the list called MESSAGE$. BASIC puts the messages into the list with the command READ.

The READ command works like this: READ looks for the word DATA. The READ statement takes the message in that DATA statement and makes it the first item in the list. The next READ statement looks for the next DATA statement. That message in quotation marks is now the second item in the list of messages. Now these variable names are ready for the program to use.

Here's one way to instruct the computer to read these 20 messages:

```
READ MESSAGE$(1)
READ MESSAGE$(2)
READ MESSAGE$(3)
READ MESSAGE$(4)
READ MESSAGE$(5)
```

and so on . . . up to MESSAGE$(20). Now that would be a lot of work to type 20 messages into one list. Can you imagine what it would be like for a list bigger than 20? Thankfully, BASIC has a shortcut you can use.

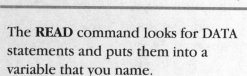

TechnoBabble

The **DATA** command contains a name or part of a list.

The **READ** command looks for DATA statements and puts them into a variable that you name.

Take a Shortcut

There is a better way to put the 8-Ball messages into the MESSAGE$ list. You can use the FOR and NEXT commands in a loop to make the job easier. (You can go back and read about FOR and NEXT in Chapter 4.) A loop really speeds up the work of putting a long list of information into an array, or list variable.

Look at lines 3700 through 3900 to see how the FOR and NEXT commands were used in the 8BALLSUB.BAS program.

```
3700 FOR COUNT = 1 TO 20
3800 READ MESSAGE$(COUNT)
3900 NEXT COUNT
```

The FOR and NEXT commands work as a team to tell the computer to repeat some lines over and over until something special happens.

1 Line 3700 tells the program to repeat the next few lines until the variable COUNT equals 20. In other words, do the next line 20 times.

2 The READ statement in line 3800 looks for the first DATA statement in the program. When the computer finds that DATA statement, the message goes into the MESSAGE$ list. The first time Message$(COUNT) is Message $(1). The second time Message$(COUNT) is Message$(2), and so on.

3 The word NEXT, in line 3900 adds 1 to COUNT, and then tells the computer to go back to the word FOR in line 3700 to repeat the process.

It takes just three lines of BASIC to load all 20 messages into the list. Whew!

Getting a Different 8-Ball Message

A real Magic 8-Ball toy shows a different message whenever the ball gets another shake. The first message that floats up against the clear window is the one you see. Each time you shake the Magic 8-Ball, each message has the same chance to float up to the window.

For the computer 8-Ball Game, you want the computer to mix up the messages, so a new one prints on the screen each time the player types a question. Then the computer game will act or seem like the real Magic 8-Ball.

TechnoBabble

Programmers use **random** numbers for many reasons. Whenever a program needs a random number, the programmer lets the computer pick one with a **RANDOM NUMBER GENERATOR**. It's almost like a mini lottery going on inside the computer. Think of a tiny person inside the computer, drawing numbers out of a basket!

The messages in the 8-Ball are **random**, which means unpredictable. It is what happens when you pick one number out of a hat that holds many numbers, or when you throw dice or pull a card out of a deck. Many games are more fun when they are unpredictable. BASIC has a handy way to pick an unpredictable choice for any game.

Creating Random Numbers

This program uses a command called **RND**, short for random. RND is used in line 6700 to give a random number between 1 and 20.

```
6500 REM Randomly choose the message from the Eight Ball
6600 RANDOMIZE TIMER
6700 ANSWER = INT(20 * RND(1)) + 1
```

Here is how to understand the math formula used in Line 6700.

1 RND tells the computer to give you any number between 0 and 1, such as .3456, .0005, or .9999.

2 You multiply this random number by 20.

3 And then you add 1.

The new number is a number between 1 and 20.

The variable, named ANSWER, now holds a random number between 1 and 20. Whatever that number is, the computer can find the message in the list of 8-Ball messages. Line 6600 uses a word called RANDOMIZE in the line right before the RND function. This word makes the computer start over each time it gives your program a new random number. That way your program will almost always get a different number.

```
7100 PRINT "The wise 8-Ball says"
7200 PRINT MESSAGE$ (ANSWER)
```

Line 7200 prints the MESSAGE$(ANSWER). ANSWER is the number of a message in the list.

So that's how you program your computer to get a different message each time.

Try This!

Let's have the computer pick a number between 1 and 52. Type in this program.

```
1. RANDOMIZE TIMER
2. CARD = INT(52*RND(1))+1
3. PRINT "The card you picked is card number  ," CARD
```

Run this program several times. See how many numbers it picks before it repeats one.

To Make a Long Story Short . . .

This chapter showed you how BASIC can handle long lists of information with a variable list called an array. An array can hold many pieces of information. The DIM command tells the computer how many elements the array will hold. You saw how to put a list of information into an array variable with a loop that uses the FOR and NEXT commands. The loop repeats a READ command, which looks for a DATA command and puts the DATA message into an array variable.

This chapter also showed you what a random number is and how it can add some surprise to your game programs. The computer can pick a random number for any program by using a random number generator.

The 8-Ball program called 8BALLSUB.BAS is a simple, funny game to play. If you study this program, you can learn to organize lists of information. You can also see how to make the computer mix up choices for other games of chance!

CHAPTER SEVEN

ONE PICTURE IS WORTH ONE THOUSAND WORDS

You are a full-grown red salmon. You gaze into the water ahead and eye an octopus. Oh dear, it looks frightening! What should you do? Quickly swim away from this creature? Or dive toward it?

One way to make an adventure game program more interesting is to add pictures. For example, the short paragraph you just read would look really good with an illustration. The OCTCOLOR.BAS program has a picture that might go really well with this story. Run the program and take a look. (If you're not sure how to run this program, see the instructions at the beginning of Chapter 3.)

How Did it Look?

So, what did you think? You've probably heard the old saying, "A picture is worth a thousand words." It's true. Pictures can really add interest to your story and make the program interesting.

This chapter will tell you how BASIC programming can add pictures to any computer program.

Is It Hard to Make Pictures?

Computer pictures are called **graphics**. Graphics are complicated and take a lot of time to create. But when you finally finish one and it works—you'll see it was worth all the effort.

The picture you try to make on your computer may look all wrong. You might get an error message that doesn't make any sense. But if it doesn't work right the first time, try—try—try again!

Be warned—once you learn a few tricks, you'll be hooked. It is so much fun to create a picture or make the screen look really neat. It's like a puzzle or game in itself to create the "look" you want.

The Screen Is Your Paper

Do you enjoy art class? Do you like to doodle? The screen is your paper now. You just need to know how to get your ideas for art onto the screen.

Your computer screen is divided up into little tiny dots. You can hardly see the dots because they are so small. These dots are called **pixels**.

TechnoBabble

Graphics is a word programmers use when they mean pictures or colors on a computer.

If you had a super-power magnifying glass, you could look at the computer screen and see these dots. The dots are all lined up in neat, tidy rows across the screen, and in neat, tidy columns up and down the screen. Without the magnifying glass, the dots are so small they just blend together, and you can't see them.

TechnoBabble

Each dot on the computer screen is called a **pixel**. (No, not "pixie"—that's an elf.) Pixel is a short way of saying *pic*ture *el*ement.

Pixels and Screens

There are three different screens full of pixels on BASIC. Each screen has a different amount of pixels it can show. You can choose these screens by using the BASIC command SCREEN. This command works in every computer program. It tells the computer which type of screen your program will use—SCREEN 0, SCREEN 1, or SCREEN 2.

Tip Offs

Not all BASIC statements work on all types of screens. If your program includes a BASIC statement that doesn't work on the type of screen you use, you will get an error when you run the program. That's why you should learn about screen types.

SCREEN 0

This is the screen you see when you first get into BASIC. SCREEN 0 has 25 rows. You can choose to make the screen either 80 or 40 columns wide. Writing looks very nice and neat in SCREEN 0. This is the best screen for looking at program lists and editing your program. BASIC **cannot** draw pictures in SCREEN 0, but you can choose from 16 colors.

SCREEN 1

This screen has 200 rows and 320 columns of pixels. You can choose from four colors. You can draw pictures or print words in SCREEN 1. Words and letters look wide and fat. This is a good screen to draw on.

SCREEN 2

This screen has 200 rows and 640 columns of pixels, so there are more pixels than SCREEN 1. Words and pictures look clearer on SCREEN 2. Only two colors are available in SCREEN 2. This is a good screen to draw on too.

Try This!

Type in this little program:

```
1 SCREEN 0
2 PRINT "Screen 0 looks like this"
```

Run the program and see what the screen looks like. Then change each 0 to a 1 and run it again. Now, change each 1 to a 2, and run it again. How did the screen change each time?

Which Pixel Is Which?

Your house has a street address that tells the mail carrier where you live. Each pixel has an address, too.

It takes two numbers to tell the address of each pixel. The first number tells the column, and the second number gives its row number. We write the pixel address with parentheses, like this: (x,y).

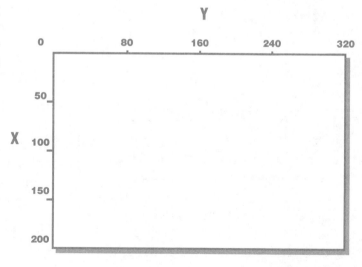

The letter *x* stands for the number of the column that runs up and down the page. The *y* stands for the number of the row that runs across the page. You may already feel comfortable with this (*x,y*) address if you studied graphing in math class.

Both *x* and *y* start from zero (0) at the top left corner of the screen. The *x* gets larger towards the bottom of the screen. The *y* gets larger towards the right of the screen.

Try This!

See if you can find these sample pixel addresses on the pixel graph. Try to put these pixels on the screen. Just make a dot at each address. You can estimate. See how close you can get.

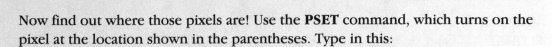

A=(80,50)   B=(240,150)   C=(160,150)

Now find out where those pixels are! Use the **PSET** command, which turns on the pixel at the location shown in the parentheses. Type in this:

```
1 SCREEN 1          4 PSET(160,150),2
2 PSET(80,50)       5 PSET(200,75),3
3 PSET(240,150),1   Now run the program.
```

The number after the parenthesis "turns on" a color. When you run this, you'll see where the pixels really are located! Did you notice which pixels were in color?

TechnoBabble

The **PSET** command "turns on" a pixel. This command uses numbers to pinpoint the location. The numbers are written in parentheses. For example, PSET (80,50) turns on a pixel located at those coordinates in the x,y screen grid.

Color Pixels to Make a Picture

All pixels on the screen start out the same color. To make a picture on the computer screen, you just color in certain pixels. The only trick is to know how to tell the computer which pixels to color—and which ones not to!

(The activity on page 87 will give you an idea of how small those pixels are.)

Circles

Working with pixels is pretty tricky. But BASIC has some drawing shortcuts. One of them is the **CIRCLE** command, which tells the computer to draw a circle. You can also draw lots of different curves if you know how to use the CIRCLE statement.

It may surprise you that the octopus picture below was drawn using circles! It uses whole circles, stretched-out circles, and parts of circles.

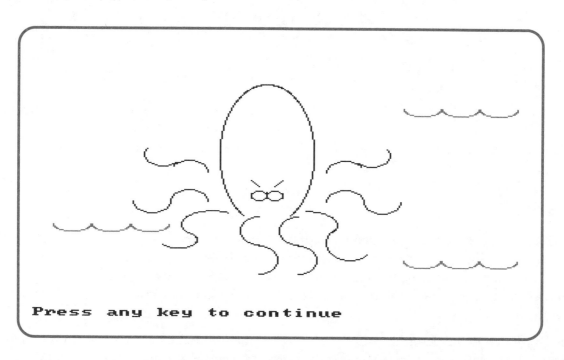

This octopus and the waves were all drawn with circles.

Before you use CIRCLE in a statement, you need to know a little bit about circles. (You probably learned about circles in your math class. Did you pay attention?) Even if it didn't make much sense in math class, you will understand circles after you work at drawing them with BASIC.

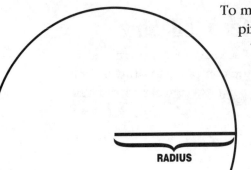

RADIUS

To make a circle, the computer needs to know which pixel is the center, and how big to make the circle. The size of the circle depends on its **radius**. The radius is the length of a line from the center out to the edge of the circle.

Eye, Eye, Sir!

Would you like to know how to draw the octopus using only circles? We'll start to draw the eyes first. Look closely at the eye of the octopus (in the computer picture shown earlier). Each eye of the octopus is a circle. Look at these three lines from the OCTCOLOR.BAS program:

```
3900 REM Eyes
4000     CIRCLE (155, 95), 5
4100     CIRCLE (145, 95), 5
```

Line number 3900 is just a comment line to tell you that the next section will draw the eyes. Do you see the number 5 at the end of two lines? The 5 is the radius of each circle. Both eyes are on the same row, number 95. These two CIRCLE statements get the job done.

Curves

It seems easy enough to most people to draw circles and curves. But have you ever tried to teach a machine how to draw those shapes? It's almost like trying to reinvent the wheel! You draw a circle using pencil and paper. You've been doing that since kindergarten. You just place the pencil point on the paper, and going counterclockwise, you draw a circle. No big deal.

Even though BASIC starts all circles and curves at the 0, we don't always have to start and stop a circle at 0. We can make interesting curves by starting the circle at other points around the circle.

Try This!

Let's color a pixel!

```
1 SCREEN 1
2 PSET (160,100)
```

Run the program. If you look—really close—right at the center of
your screen, you will see one tiny pixel is white. That gives you an idea
of how tiny those pixels really are.

Now change line 2 to look like this:

```
2 PSET (160,100),2
```

It's the same statement—just add `,2` to the end. When you run this, the 2 changes
the color of that pixel. Try to see what happens if you try 1 or 3.

Here is an experiment with a radius. Try this on your computer. Type in this
program:

```
1 SCREEN 1
2 CIRCLE (160,100),5
```

Run the program to see what happens. You should see a circle drawn on the
screen. The numbers `(160,100)` are the (x,y) address for the center of the screen.

Now, move the cursor to the 5 at the end of line 2, and change it to `60`. This
changes the radius of the circle to 60. Run the program again and see what
happens.

BASIC draws curves sort of like you did in the last activity, but not quite as easily.
BASIC uses a starting point and ending point on the circle, just as you do in the
activities. The computer wants you to name those two points on the circle as an
angle in **radians**. (Yikes! This sounds dangerous!)

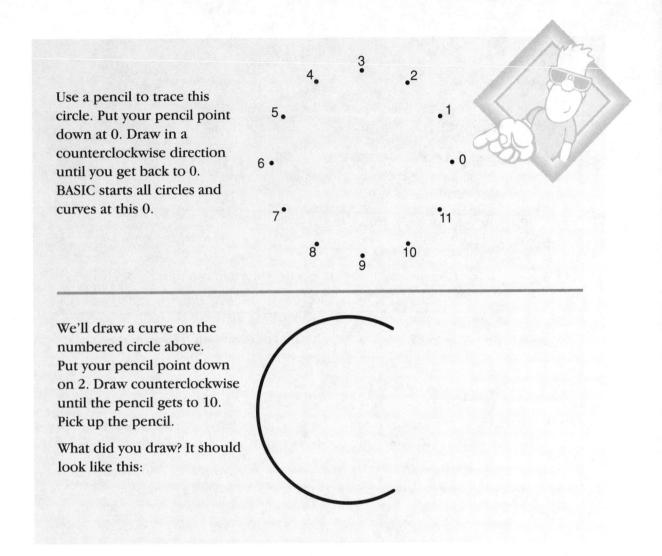

Use a pencil to trace this circle. Put your pencil point down at 0. Draw in a counterclockwise direction until you get back to 0. BASIC starts all circles and curves at this 0.

We'll draw a curve on the numbered circle above. Put your pencil point down on 2. Draw counterclockwise until the pencil gets to 10. Pick up the pencil.

What did you draw? It should look like this:

This next diagram shows the same points you saw in the last activity, except there are some strange formulas. These points are measured in radians. I know they look like odd formulas to most people, but this is how they need to be.

$4^{PI}\!/_6$ • $3^{PI}\!/_6$ • $2^{PI}\!/_6$ •

Now look at this program line that draws the octopus body:

```
3800 CIRCLE (150, 60), 60, ,
10 * PI / 6, 8 * PI / 6, 2
```

$5^{PI}\!/_6$ • $1^{PI}\!/_6$ •

Two math formulas have been used. These two math formulas show the starting point and ending point for the circle that makes up the octopus body:

$6^{PI}\!/_6$ •   • 0

10 * PI / 6 figures out the starting point for the circle.

$7^{PI}\!/_6$ • $11^{PI}\!/_6$ •

$8^{PI}\!/_6$ • $10^{PI}\!/_6$ • $9^{PI}\!/_6$ •

8 * PI / 6 figures out the ending point for the circle.

Let's talk about this formula called PI.

What Is PI, Anyway?

In a basic program, pi is not made out of pastry dough and fruit—that would be "pie." **Pi** is a special number used in calculating circles. You may recognize it as π. So why is BASIC using pi?

BASIC measures the points all around the circle (and names them) as angles in radians. You might be used to measuring angles in degrees, but BASIC wants these angles measured in radians. To measure in radians, you need to use a special number called pi.

Pi never changes. If you took a circle's circumference (distance around) and divided it by its diameter (the length of a line that cuts it exactly in half), you'd always get pi. Pi equals 3.14159265. The number turns out the same no matter what the measurements of a circle are. (You might want to ask your math teacher more about it).

Instead of writing out this number each time you want to use it, you can tell BASIC to use a variable called PI to hold the number. Then you just use PI when you need the actual number for pi.

But when you use the variable called PI, you must always tell the computer what the variable PI is equal to. Add a statement like this before you ever use the variable PI:

```
PI = 4 x ATN(1)
```

TechnoBabble

Radians are a measurement of how much of a circle will be drawn. It's like finding out how big your "slice of pie" will be.

Pi is a special number used for calculating circles.

This statement calculates the special number called PI. Be sure to put a statement like this near the beginning of your program, before the lines where PI is used in a formula.

Stretch Your Circles into Other Shapes

The circles we've studied so far don't really look like an octopus body. The circles are too round—too "circular!" An octopus needs a longer and skinnier body. The CIRCLE statement needs one more piece of information if we want to change the shape of the curve. It is at the very end of the line.

```
3800 CIRCLE (150, 60), 60, , 10 * PI / 6, 8 * PI / 6, 2
```

When that last number is more than 1, the circle stretches up and down. When that last number is less than 1, the circle stretches sideways.

The higher the number, the more stretched the circle will become. The lower the number, the fatter the circle will become. The octopus needs a tall, long body, so that number is 2 in line 3800.

You can really have some fun when you experiment with starting point, ending point, and that last number which stretches the circle.

Try This!

Type this in:

```
1 SCREEN 1
2 CIRCLE (100, 40), 20
```

Run this little program. It draws a circle with radius of 20. Now change line 2 to look like this:

```
2 CIRCLE (100, 40),20, , , ,2
```

Be sure to put in the right number of commas! The two lines are almost the same— except we added the 2 at the end. When you run the program, this change stretches the circle up and down.

Now try the same line, but change the last 2 to .2. Run the program again. Do you see the difference?

Curves Are Circles, Too—Sort Of!

Look at the octopus drawing again:

Do you see how curvy the octopus arms are? We made each arm with two CIRCLE statements. Study these lines from the program:

```
4400 REM BOTTOM ARM ON RIGHT
4500 CIRCLE (170, 125), 12, , PI / 2, 3 * PI / 2, 1
4600 CIRCLE (170, 150), 12, , 3 * PI / 2, PI / 2, 1
```

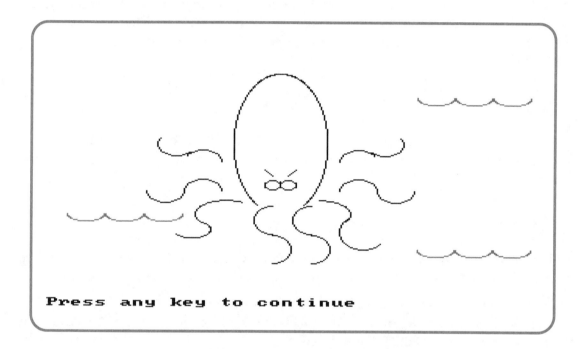

```
Press any key to continue
```

Each of these CIRCLE statements makes a part of a circle. These parts are close enough to touch each other, so together they look like one curvy arm. To make this work, you have to experiment with the center position, the radius, the starting and ending point, and the stretch number on the end of the CIRCLE statement.

Tip Offs

A complete circle measures 2 times pi radians around.

Making Waves

Even the waves are made with the CIRCLE statement. That CIRCLE statement is tucked inside a routine that repeats the CIRCLE statement 3 times. Study these lines:

```
1900 REM Wave A
2000 FOR WAVE = 250 TO 300 STEP 25
2100   CIRCLE (WAVE, 20), 12, 1, PI, 0, .5
2200 NEXT WAVE
```

The variable, named WAVE, holds the column number for the center of the circle. The FOR and NEXT statements repeat the CIRCLE statement 3 times. The 3 circles are close enough to touch. The pattern they make looks like a wave. (Chapter 6 showed you how to use FOR and NEXT commands.)

Whew!

Drawing pictures is a complicated job. It takes a lot of practice to get it right. Just be patient. Remember to study the examples in this chapter to help you build your own graphics.

To Make a Long Story Short . . .

Figuring out how to make pictures on the computer screen is like a game in itself. There are several BASIC statements that let you draw circles, boxes, lines, and curves.

This chapter showed you how to color one pixel on a computer screen using the PSET command. There are 3 different ways the pixels are lined up on the screen. You can draw pictures when you use SCREENTYPES 1 and 2.

We looked at how BASIC draws a circle and curve. The challenging part of drawing curves is to name the starting and ending point of a curve with a math formula. That formula calculates a point on a circle that is really an angle measured in radians. We included a chart to help you know some points all around the circle. You can draw a lot of curves with these 12 points.

CHAPTER EIGHT

LIGHTS, CAMERA, ACTION!

You gaze into the water ahead and see—an octopus! It looks menacing! What should you do? Quickly swim away from the creature? Or dive toward it?

Not to worry—it's actually a Pacific Ocean octopus, and they grow to be only three inches long. It is a peaceful creature, and would not hurt any human. But it may fight back when you attack it, because you are a red salmon. You can eat this poor little octopus for dinner!

In the last chapter, you learned a little about drawing graphics using BASIC. In this chapter, you'll learn how to draw lines and add color and motion to your BASIC pictures. The programming adventure sample about the salmon and the octopus is a good way to show you how.

The beginning paragraph of the adventure needs a picture of a mean octopus that looks like it could, and would, eat a small salmon. When the story goes on and it turns out the octopus is smaller than the salmon, then we need a picture of a scared-looking octopus. How do we change the octopus drawing? All it takes is changing a few lines. Keep reading and you'll find some great tips for changing your computer drawings.

Line Up!

First let's talk about straight lines. BASIC is very good at drawing nice, straight lines. BASIC can make straight lines go in every direction. Lines can be long, short, or any length. Is it any surprise that BASIC uses the word DRAW to draw a line?

Pretend the computer screen is really a great big, blank parking lot. There are no lines or markings on the lot at all. A paint machine is ready to paint whatever you want all over that parking lot. You can use the BASIC **draw commands** to tell the machine which direction to go, what color paint to use, when to put the brush on the surface, and when to lift it up.

DRAW is easy to use. Take a look at the list of DRAW commands.

DRAW commands

Un Draw up
Dn Draw down
Ln Draw left
Rn Draw right

En Draw diagonally up and right
Fn Draw diagonally down and right
Gn Draw diagonally down and left
Hn Move diagonally up and left
B   Raise pen (move without drawing)
N   Move, but return to where pen started
TAn Turn angle of DRAW statements (*n* is the angle, in degrees)
Pn Paint color (*n* is one of several color codes)

All of the *n*'s in these commands are numbers you'll put in to tell the commands how far (in pixels) to go each time.

You can draw lots of different pictures with the word DRAW and all those DRAW commands. You don't even have to have a great talent for art. It does take lots of practice, though. Try this next activity to see what you can do.

Try This!

Type in and run this program. It draws a triangle and fills it in with color. (The messages at the end of each line are comments about that line. Type those in, too!)

```
1 SCREEN 1
2 DRAW "BR-20 BD-50"        'Move to center of screen
3 DRAW "F60 L120 E60"       'Draws a triangle
4 DRAW "BD20"               'Moves pen to inside triangle
5 DRAW "P2,3"               'Fills triangle with color
```

See if you can figure out how each of the lines in the program works. If you want, you type in line 1 and just one other line after that—this gives you a two-line program. If you run it, you'll see what each new line actually does on the screen.

Faces Tell a Story

Let's study some more DRAW commands in action. Are you good at drawing faces? Faces are funny. (Not yours, of course!) The faces you draw with BASIC can show a lot of personality.

Look at the next picture of a boy with a great hairstyle. Okay, maybe not great. Maybe he should try a different barber. (Or maybe a better artist.) At least you can see how the DRAW statement works to make straight lines. (The program that draws this is called BOY.BAS and it's on the disk.)

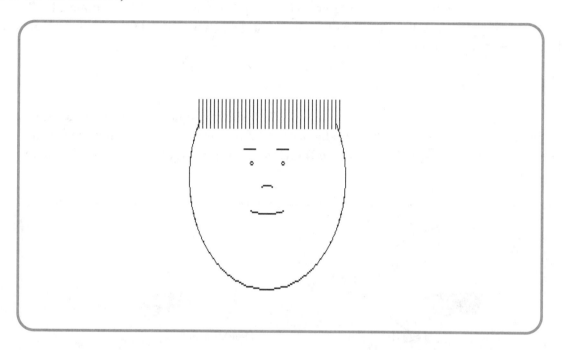

This boy's hair was drawn with the DRAW command.

So how did BASIC draw this boy? Read the programming lines to find out:

```
1100 REM Hair ******************************************
1200 PSET (212, 65) 'Places marker at top left of boy's head
1300 HAIR$ = "NU20 BR5"
1400  FOR MOVE = 1 TO 37
1500    DRAW HAIR$
1600  NEXT MOVE
```

This boy has 37 strands of hair. We don't want to make 37 DRAW statements in a program. Instead, Line number 1300 puts the drawing commands in a variable called HAIR$. Study the DRAW commands written next to the variable. Can you figure out what they mean? (Use the DRAW commands chart.)

Now we just put the DRAW statement in a FOR...NEXT loop. The computer keeps track of how many times the DRAW statement goes, and stops after 37 repeats.

Now that wasn't so bad, was it?

The first command is N. It tells the pen to come back to where it started when it's finished drawing. The U20 command tells the pen to draw up 20 pixels. The BR5 command tells the pen to stop drawing and move over 5 pixels. And of course, our FOR...NEXT command tells the computer to repeat this 37 times.

Filling Areas In

Now let's see how to use the paint command. We'll show you how it's done on a baby face. Why would we want to draw a baby? Why not? They are kind of cute—sometimes. And since we haven't yet learned about using BASIC to create sound, the babies in this chapter can't cry!

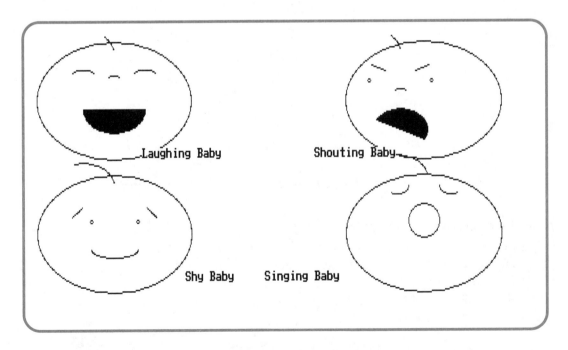

Aren't you glad we haven't learned how to program sounds yet?

Study these program lines for the laughing baby.

```
2600 DRAW "BG5"      'Moves pointer inside of baby's mouth
2700 DRAW "P1,2"     'Colors baby's mouth
```

One of the drawing commands you can use with the DRAW statement fills any area with your choice of color. That's what makes the laughing baby's smile stand out. The B moves the marker inside the half circle of the baby's mouth. The P paints that area until it reaches the edge of the mouth.

Subroutines also helped draw these babies in the picture. You can take a look at all the program lines used on the baby drawings by looking at the BABY.BAS program on the disk.

Now that you've read about DRAW commands and how they work, let's see what they could do for our octopus story.

Is the Octopus Scared or Scary?

Remember our octopus and salmon story? Let's look at the octopus and see how to make him both scary and scared. You don't have to be an artist to change the expression of the octopus. The only difference is the way the eyebrows are drawn.

Study the line listing from the OCTCOLOR.BAS program to see how both versions are drawn:

```
9900 REM Eyebrows:
10000 REM Angry
10100 REM PSET (150, 92) 'Position for next DRAW statements
10200 REM DRAW "BE5 E5 BG10 BH5 H5" 'Angry
10300 REM   'Worried
10400    PSET (150, 65)    'Position for next DRAW statements
10500    DRAW "BF5 F5 BH10 BG5 G5"  'Worried
10600    PRESET (150, 65)  'Hide the point
10700 RETURN
10800 REM End routine ****************************************
10900 END
```

The REM statements tell you which octopus expression is which. The program for eyebrows—for both types of octopus—starts with the word PSET. PSET moves the cursor to the place on the screen where the eyebrow should start. Then the DRAW command—in the next line—tells the computer to start drawing.

The angry eyebrow starts low; the scared eyebrow starts higher. Do you see those two (x,y) positions in lines 10100 and 10400? These are the locations of the pixels on the computer screen.

And here's how the octopus pictures turned out:

How would you like to meet up with this octopus?

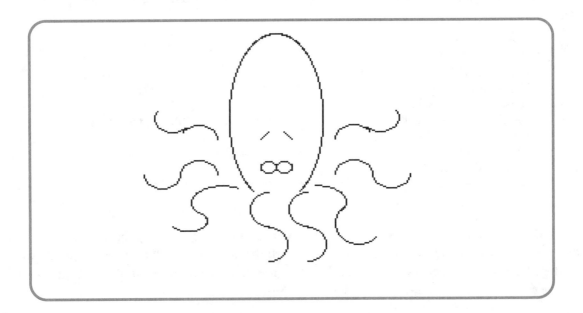

This octopus doesn't look so threatening now!

Color

How about adding some color to the octopus? We can give the little guy a more colorful scene by adding color to his ocean. Black-and-white is fine, but BASIC gives you several colors to brighten up your pictures. You can change the background color, the pen color, or fill special areas with color.

Background Color

BASIC uses the word **COLOR** to change the color over the entire screen. Look how easy this command is:

```
1400 COLOR 0      'Background color of ocean
```

Line number 1400 controls the color of the ocean in the program, with the BASIC word COLOR.

The number 0 is a color code that happens to be black. Here is a list of the color codes you can use with the word COLOR to change the background screen color:

0	Black
1	Blue
2	Green
3	Cyan (pale blue)
4	Red
5	Magenta
6	Brown
7	White
8	Gray
9	Light blue
10	Light green
11	Light cyan
12	Light red
13	Light magenta
14	Yellow
15	Bright white

TechnoBabble

The **COLOR** command adds color to the screen.

What is **cyan**? It sounds like a robot warrior from a Saturday morning cartoon! It really is a greenish-blue color. How about Magenta? Wasn't he a famous Portuguese explorer in the 15th century? No, that was Magellan. **Magenta** is a deep purplish-red color in the "land of computers."

Type and run this program to see the colors you can choose from on your screen.

```
1 SCREEN 1
2 CLS
3 FOR SHADE = 0 TO 14
4    COLOR SHADE
5    PRINT "This is Color Code ";SHADE
6 NEXT SHADE
```

Drawing Colors

As we've seen, the COLOR command changes the **background color** of the screen. BASIC also lets you add a color choice for the pictures you draw with the pen and paint commands.

These are the "pen" color codes.

Color	Code
Black	0
Cyan	1
Magenta	2
White	3

What happens if you use a black pen on a black screen? Or a magenta pen on a magenta screen? Invisible ink! Watch out for that problem. If you ever lose your pen in the background, simply end the program by holding down the Ctrl key while you press the Break key.

Take a look at how color is used in these sample lines from the OCTCOLOR.BAS program:

```
1800 REM Background:
1900 REM Wave A
2000 FOR WAVE = 250 TO 300 STEP 25
2100    CIRCLE (WAVE, 20), 12, 1, PI, 0, .5
```

The CIRCLE statement leaves a space for a color code, right after the radius at the end of the line. The waves in the octopus picture are really half-circles that use color number 1 blue.

In real life, when an octopus becomes frightened, it can change its own color. We could change this guy's color by drawing him again with a different color code. You can see how color makes adventure games more interesting.

Move It!

You've learned how to draw it and color it but now it's time to move it. Hang on to your seats—because we are going to learn how to make a drawing move around the screen. That's called **animation**!

To see how this works, stop and run the ANIMOCTI.BAS program from your disk or hard drive. (If you're not sure how to run this, see the instructions at the beginning of Chapter 3).

Wow!

How was that? Wouldn't your program look great if the pictures could move? You can make any picture move across the screen.

Here's how the process works:

1. Draw the picture on the screen, and save it like a snapshot or photograph.

2. Erase the picture from the screen.

3. Draw the same picture in a new place on the screen and save it.

4. Erase the old picture from the screen.

5. Repeat the whole process several times.

Believe it or not, these steps make any drawing seem to move.

Say Cheese?

The ANIMOCTI.BAS program you just ran draws the octopus on the screen using CIRCLE commands. (You learned about CIRCLE commands in Chapter 7.) The next step to start to move the octopus is to "take a picture" of it. You can do this with a GET command.

Using (x,y) coordinates that tell the computer what part of the screen to take a "snapshot" of, the GET command then saves the "snapshot." It stores this "snapshot" in a list variable (array).

Take a look at this GET command line from the ANIMOCTI.BAS program:

```
6900 GET (50,0)-(240,175), IMAGE 'store snapshot in Image
7000 CLS
```

Notice the (x,y) coordinates after the word GET in line 6900. Those tell the command what part of the screen to take a picture of. The word IMAGE in line 6900 is the name of the variable where the "snapshot" will be stored. When the picture is saved, line 7000 clears the screen (CLS).

Now that GET has got a picture of your drawing, you're ready to make it move.

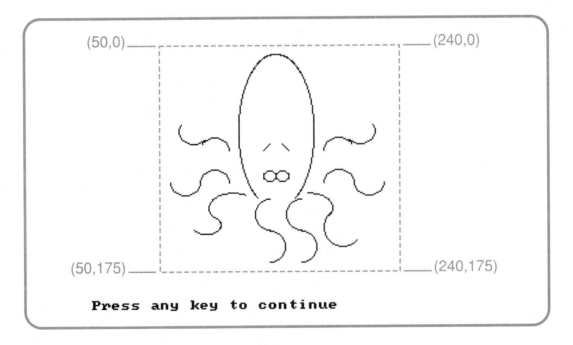

After the GET command saves this snapshot, the program clears the screen with CLS.

Move the Snapshot

Study lines 7900 through 9700 to see how the octopus picture moves.

```
7900 REM Go forward:
8000   FOR X = 25 TO 100 STEP 5
8100     GOSUB 9000     'GOSUB Go octopus
8200   NEXT X
8300 RETURN
9000 REM Go octopus:
9200     PUT (X, 0), IMAGE
9300      NOW! = TIMER        'Pause the action
9400      WHILE TIMER > NOW! + .15 'for .15 second
9500      WEND
9600     PUT (X, 0), IMAGE
9700 RETURN
```

Lines 7900 through 9700 go through the steps to make the snapshot seem to move across the screen.

The **PUT** command is used to show the picture on the screen. Look at line 9200. This instruction tells the computer to get the picture out of the variable named IMAGE (remember, variables are like holding boxes) and make it appear on the screen.

The second PUT command, used in line 9600, erases the picture. The good old FOR and NEXT commands, in lines 8000 and 8200, give new positions for the picture each time it is drawn.

And finally, the TIMER command in lines 9200 to 9500 slows down the picture so you can see it better as it moves across the screen.

If all of this seems pretty complicated to you, don't worry—it is! The best way to learn animation is to experiment through trial and error.

TechnoBabble

The **GET** command is used to store a snapshot of a picture drawn on the screen. Used with the **PUT** command, the program makes an animated (or moving) picture. The PUT command draws a stored picture on the screen wherever you tell it to with x, y coordinates.

Shake the 8-Ball

Remember the 8-Ball game in Chapter 6? Try running the 8BALLPIC.BAS program that came on the disk. (If you need help running this program, see the instructions at the beginning of Chapter 3.) This program will show you an animated 8-Ball.

Did it Work?

Now study the program listing to see how we made the 8-Ball picture move.

```
12800 REM Shake the Ball:
12900   NOW! = TIMER
13000   WHILE TIMER < NOW! + 2          'About 25 seconds
13100   REM The ball seems to move back and forth
13200       PUT (75, 10), IMAGE
13300       PUT (75, 10), IMAGE
13400       PUT (95, 10), IMAGE
13500       PUT (95, 10), IMAGE
13600   WEND
13700 RETURN
```

The subroutine, in lines 12800 through 13700, takes the picture from the array variable named IMAGE and moves it back and forth. It moves it between the x=75 pixel and the x=95 pixel.

The first PUT command, in line 13200, makes the picture show up. The next PUT command, in line 13300, erases it. Then the picture is moved over and shown again in line 13400. All of this makes the 8-Ball seem to shake.

The TIMER command slows the program down so you can see the picture briefly before it's erased again.

Whew! This drawing stuff is a lot of work!

Print with Cool Symbols

Your computer has some neat little built-in pictures that you can print on the screen, even when the computer is in SCREEN 0 mode.

Look in Appendix B for a list of these little pictures and the code for each one. Try this next activity to see what some of them look like.

Try This!

Type in this little program and run it.

```
1 PRINT "I ";CHR$(3);" Summer Vacation ";CHR$(15)
```

You'll see an example of how these pictures can be used.

These pictures are called **ASCII** characters. When you use the right code in the CHR$(*x*) command, you can print one of these characters on your screen. You'll learn more about how to use these pictures in Appendix B.

Tip Offs

Remember that the DRAW and CIRCLE statements do not work in SCREEN 0 because it is designed for words only, not pictures.

Combine Symbols and Graphics

You can draw using just these special ASCII pictures. But you can also combine them with the graphics you draw with CIRCLE or DRAW. This next illustration of a little worm is made of circles, but his antennae are really parentheses! He is drawn by the WORM.BAS program on your disk.

Let's hope this isn't a bookworm—it might get hungry!

Look at these two lines from the WORM.BAS program:

```
185 LOCATE 12,59
190 PRINT CHR$(41);" ";CHR$(40)
```

The LOCATE command in line 185 tells the computer where to put the parentheses on the screen. They will be drawn at row 12, column 59.

Line 190 provides the antennas. CHR$(41) and CHR$(40) are the codes that tell the computer to print the parentheses. Pretty easy, huh?

To Make a Long Story Short . . .

T his chapter showed you how to draw lines and add color to your pictures. The word COLOR changes the background color of the screen or adds color to your picture.

You also learned a little about animation—making your pictures seem to move.

Learning to draw with BASIC takes lots of time, patience, and practice. But it's also a lot of fun!

CHAPTER NINE
THE SOUND OF MUSIC

Danger lurks nearby. Is it the slime monster? Could it be the strange Gypsy woman, or some unknown, horrible creature that's waiting for you? Listen carefully for a clue!

It's too bad you can't hear this book as you read it. But since books like this can't make sounds, you'll just have to imagine how a scary song would sound in the background of an adventure game like the one you just read.

Adding sound is another way to make your program interesting. In this chapter, we're going to experiment with the music BASIC can make on your computer. It's not too hard to make music with the computer. Do you have a song in your head? You can play it on your computer if you know the right notes.

You can program your own original songs to play on your computer. Or, you can program a sheet of music someone else composed. We'll go over both ways of getting your computer to turn into an instrument!

The Language of Music

Before you can program BASIC to make songs, you must know about another language called *music*. Yes, that's right! Music has a language all its own.

If you already know how to read and understand music, then it will be simple for you to understand how to program your computer to play music. If you do not know very much about music, we'll go over some step-by-step examples to show you how to add songs to your program. Also, you can get help from a music teacher or a friend who understands music.

Musical Notes

On the next page, you will see a picture of a piano keyboard. The keys are labeled with musical notes. Every key on the piano keyboard makes a different note. BASIC uses the same names for notes as musicians do.

White Keys

A musician calls the white keys C, D, E, F, G, A, and B. BASIC calls each set of seven white notes, starting with C, an **octave**. BASIC assumes a note is in the fourth octave (middle notes on the piano), unless you tell it differently. We'll show you how in a little while.

Black Keys

The black keys are also labeled with letters, and with a + or – symbol. The + means the key is a **sharp** key. That means it is a little higher than the white note to its left.

The – means the key is a **flat**. A flat key is a little lower than the white note to its right. Sometimes a black note is both a sharp and a flat. Look at the key between C and D. It can be called either C-sharp or D-flat.

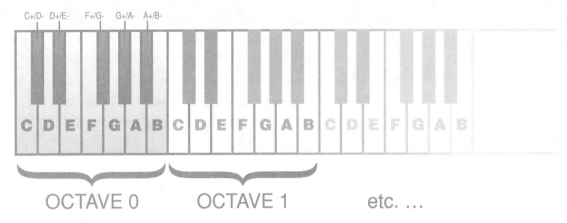

BASIC uses the PLAY command to play music. Now that you know the names of the notes, let's learn how to play them on the computer!

Try This!

Type in this line.

```
10 PLAY "C C G G A A G F F E E D D D D C"
```

Run this one-line program to listen to the song.

Does it sound funny? Can you recognize it as "The Alphabet Song"?

Keep reading to find out how to make it sound better!
(Don't clear your screen; we'll use this line in the next activity.)

Hold That Note!

There is more to a song than just the sounds of notes. Songs sound better when some notes are played longer than other notes.

Musicians use different terms for notes that are different lengths. Imagine someone beating a drum in a steady rhythm. A note that lasts for four drum beats called a **whole note.** A note that lasts two beats is called a **half note.** And a note that lasts only one beat is called a **quarter note.** BASIC uses L1 for whole notes, L2 for half notes, and L4 for quarter notes. BASIC assumes a note is a quarter note unless you tell it otherwise by using L1 or L2. The next activity lets you add the note length to the alphabet song.

TechnoBabble

The **PLAY** command is used to tell the computer to play sound.

Try This!

We're going to add another line to the program in the last activity. (Is it still on your screen?) Add a line 20 below line 10 that looks like this:

```
20 PLAY "L2C C G G A A L1G L2F F E E L4D D D D L1C"
```

Now run this changed program to listen to the tune. First the old way will play in line 10, then line 20 will play the new way. Which sounds better?

Now you know how to write your own musical ideas in a BASIC program. Next we'll learn how to take music notes on paper and make them into a BASIC program.

Changing Sheet Music to BASIC

A composer writes music on paper so that musicians can read it and play it on instruments. You can see two lines of music in the picture below. The song is "Mary Had a Little Lamb."

You've probably seen music written like this before. A musician knows what notes to play because each one is written on a certain line.

The black notes are quarter notes, and the white notes are half notes. The dot at the end of line 2 means to hold that half note for one more beat.

The next activity shows you how to write this song in BASIC for your computer. If you do not know the names of musical notes or how to read music, this is where you will need some help from a friend or teacher who does know the length and names of notes. You'll need to write down on notebook paper the name of each note and its length.

Once you know the names of the notes and how long each note should be played, then you can put the song into BASIC, using the PLAY command.

Try This!

Type these lines.

```
10 PLAY "E D C D E E L2E L4D D L2D L4E G L2G"
20 PLAY "L4E D C D E E E E D D E D L2C."
```

Now, run this program.

If you typed the lines correctly, your computer should play the first part of "Mary Had a Little Lamb."

Here's how the "Mary Had a Little Lamb" sheet music was turned into BASIC codes. (Study the sheet music on the previous page as you read this paragraph.) Since BASIC assumes notes are quarter notes and this song begins with quarter notes, you don't have to use the L4 at first.

1.   The first note is E (a quarter note).

2.   Then comes D, C, D, E, E (all quarter notes).

3.   Then you get to the half-note E. Write that as L2E.

4.   Next comes two quarter notes that are both Ds. You just have to write the new change in note length *once*, like this: L4D D.

5.   Then you come to another half note, so write L2D.

Can you figure out the rest? Are you wondering how to write the last note of this song? It is a dotted half-note C. Write it like this: **L2C.**. The **.** gives it the extra length, just as the dot in music gives any note its extra length.

Play It Again, BASIC!

Take a look at this program listing for a song.

Tip Offs

Use the **L** command whenever the length of a note is different from that of the note before it. Once you change the length of a note, all the notes after it will be the same length—until you change the length again.

```
10 REM Program GYPSYTUN.BAS                'Gypsy Dance by G. Verdi
20 LINE1$ = "MB O4 E C E C <L2A. L4 A B > C D < B A A A P4> "
30 LINE2$ = "MB O4 E C E C <L2A. L4 A B > C D < B A A A >A"
40 LINE3$ = "MB O4 G F E D C C C A G F E D C C L2e. L4"
50 PLAY LINE1$
60 PLAY LINE2$
70 PLAY LINE3$
80 PLAY LINE1$
90 END
```

You'll find this song already programmed on the disk that came with this book. It's named GYPSYTUN.BAS. Try running it to see how it sounds. (If you need help in running this program, see the instructions for running at the beginning of Chapter 3.)

Ah, The Sounds of Music

Did you run the GYPSYTUN.BAS? You can use BASIC music commands to play just about any kind of music, except maybe heavy metal.

There are a few more things to know about programming music with BASIC. Keep reading.

Lines 50 through 80 in the listing above tell the computer to PLAY the notes in the variables named LINE1$, LINE2$, and LINE3$. Here's a trick. It just so happens that in this song, the 4th verse sounds just like the first verse. A lot of songs are like that. Instead of setting up another variable for the 4th line, just tell the computer to play LINE1$ whenever the 4th line of music should play.

Which Octave Is This?

Let's look closer at the GYPSYTUN.BAS program listing on the previous page. There are some new symbols to learn about. Let's find out what < and > mean.

Tip Offs

Another way to switch to a new octave is to use O, (not zero), with a number to show which octave you mean.

Unless you tell it otherwise, BASIC always plays notes in octave 4. But sometimes, your music needs the notes in the other octaves to make the song sound right. If your music needs a note one octave below octave 4 (octave 3), use the < symbol to change octaves in the program.

If you need a note 2 octaves below octave 4 (octave 2), use <<, (one < for each octave).

To help you understand the octave symbols, try the next activity.

Try This!

Type in this line. Notice that it does not tell the computer which octave, or set of seven notes, to play.

```
10 REM  "C D E F G A B C D E F G A B C D E F G "
```

Run this program and listen to this music. It should sound like it keeps starting over at the same note.

Now change line 10 to look like this line. To do this, just add O2, which stands for octave 2, at the beginning, and insert > in two places.

```
10 REM PLAY "O2 C D E F G A B >C D E F G A B >C D E F G "
```

When you run this line, it should sound like it starts on the left side of the keyboard, with the low sounding notes, and keeps going higher. That's how octaves work.

Let's Take a Rest!

No, not a rest like a nap. Who wants to sleep, anyway? Learning computer music is too exciting to even think about sleeping right now.

We are talking about a *musical* rest—a little pause in a song. The musical symbols for a rest look like this:

BASIC uses a P, which stands for pause, to add a rest to a song.

Whole Rest   Half Rest   Quarter Rest

- P4 is a quarter rest (1 beat).

- P2 is a half rest (2 beats).

- P1 is a whole rest (4 beats).

Try the following activity to hear for yourself how important a little rest can be!

Try This!

Type in this line for the song "Jingle Bells:"

```
10 PLAY "E E E P4 E E E P4 E G C P4 L8D L4E"
```

Run this to hear the song.

Now type in the same line, but leave out the P4's. (There are 3 of them.)

```
10 PLAY "E E E    E E E    E G C    L8D L4E"
```

Run this new program to hear Jingle Bells without the musical rests. Which sounds better?

Don't Forget Those Black Keys

So far, all the examples have used the white key notes only. These notes are called **natural**. The black notes are useful, too. They are called **accidentals**, even when you use them on purpose! (And you thought computer programming language was weird.)

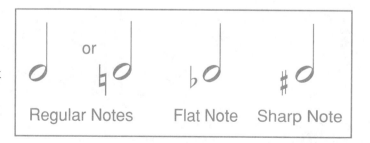

Regular Notes   Flat Note   Sharp Note

The black notes play a tone in between the natural notes. BASIC uses the symbol + (plus) to show a sharp note, and the symbol – (minus) to show a flat note. Try the next activity to hear all the notes on the keyboard.

Try This!

Step 1.

Type in this line to play eight natural notes. These are the white keys starting at octave 4, note C. The blank spaces do not change the sound.

```
10 PLAY "O4 C    D   E F   G    A    B > C"
'White keys only
```

Run this program to hear the musical **scale**.

Step 2.

Now type in this next line. This line is the same as line 10, but you're filling in those blank spaces with the name of the notes that fall on the black keys. These are called **sharp notes**.

```
20 PLAY "O4 C C+ D D+ E F F+ G G+ A A+ B > C"
'Black and white keys
```

Run this changed program to hear every note.

Step 3.

Add this next line. The black notes now can be called **flat notes**.

```
30 PLAY "O4 C D- D E- E F G- G A- A B- B > C"
'Black and white keys
```

The music in line 30 will now sound exactly like line 20! Can you figure out why?

Background Music

The PLAY statement plays a song while the computer waits. After the song finishes, the program moves on to the next instruction in the program. But while the song plays, the computer will not do anything else.

What if you want the music to play *while* the computer continues the program? What if you want some background music, like movies have?

BASIC can play background music while other parts of the program go on. The next section shows you how to use a short program to add background music to any computer game.

BASIC uses the words **ON PLAY** to let your program play music while the rest of your game goes on. ON PLAY keeps up to 32 musical notes of the song in a special area of the computer's memory and plays it over and over again until the end of the program.

Study this program listing from the BCKMUSIC.BAS sample that came on the disk.

```
20000 REM Program BCKMUSIC.BAS  Add background music to any program
20100 REM     Change Line 21400 for tune, then add as subroutine to
20150 REM     other programs
20200 ON PLAY(5) GOSUB 21300 'PlayMore Trap when 5 notes are left
20300 PLAY ON
20400 PLAY "MB"                    'Turn on Background Music
20500 GOSUB 21300              'Start the tune
20600 SCREEN 1
20700 FOR COUNTER = 1 TO 3000 'Makes a design on screen while you
20800     X = RND * 320         'listen and test music or sound
20900     Y = RND * 200
21000     PSET (X, Y)
21100 NEXT COUNTER
21200 END                   'Change this to RETURN in big program
21300 REM PlayMore:   'This line of music will play in background
21400     LINE1$ = "L1 N3 L2 N4 P4 L1 N3 L2 N4 P4 L1 N3 L2 N4 P4 L1
      N3 L2 N4"
21500     PLAY LINE1$
21600  RETURN
```

This little program plays some scary background music. Try running it to hear for yourself.

You can use this same program when you're ready to add your own music to an adventure game.

Here's how:

1. Put the codes for the song you want to play into line number 21400. (You can use LINE$ as your variable just like we did.) Make sure your song is less than 32 notes. Your song should also go along with your game, whether it's scary, peppy, or whatever.

▶2 Test the program to make sure the song sounds right. (Line numbers 20700–21100 cause dots to fill up the screen while you listen and test your music.)

▶3 When everything sounds good, merge the program with your own adventure game program. Carefully follow the directions in Chapter 5 on how to add a subroutine program to the main program.

Once you've merged this program, you'll need to make these changes to your main program:

▶1 Near the beginning of your adventure game main program, put in a line like this:

```
150 GOSUB  line number XXXXX        'Background Music
```

(Fill in XXXXX to be the line number where you start the background music subroutine.)

▶2 Delete lines 20600–21100 in the subroutine. They are only useful for testing. They print dots all over the screen while you test the song.

▶3 Change line number 21200 to read RETURN.

To Make a Long Story Short . . .

Music can add lots of interest to your program. Learn the note codes and use the PLAY and ON PLAY statements in BASIC to create your own sounds.

PLAY tells the computer to play whatever musical notes are in quotation marks.

ON PLAY tells the computer to play the music in the background while the program continues.

You can use the BCKMUSIC.BAS program to add background music to your own adventure game programs. Have fun!

CHAPTER TEN

THE ADVENTURE CONTINUES

Now that you've read this book. . .

■ You've seen what programming with BASIC can do.

■ You've studied the sample program listings in each chapter.

■ You've learned about the different BASIC commands.

What Do You Do Next?

You're ready to start programming on your own! Try building an adventure game. There are lots of programs on the disk that came with this book that you can use and combine. And of course, there are lots of good ideas for programs that no one has thought of yet.

To get you started, there are some appendices at the back of this book that can help you out.

The best way to learn BASIC programming is to practice—practice—practice.

Share the Fun with a Friend!

If you liked learning about computers and programming in this book, chances are that some of your friends will like it, too. Look for someone who can share in the fun of programming a computer. A teacher or parent might enjoy working on a program with you. Do you think you could teach your brother or sister how to make a program?

Take a Class

Have you learned the basics of BASIC programming? Do you feel like you're getting more advanced? Then you should check out classes in programming.

Some of the classes will be for adults. The adults probably won't mind if you join them in discovering more about computer programming.

Does your school offer a class in programming? Even if your school doesn't, there may be a teacher who knows BASIC. A lot of adults learned BASIC in high school or college. They might be surprised when you tell them BASIC is still a fun and easy way to play with a computer.

Read a Book

This book doesn't cover all the neat things that BASIC can do. Some of the BASIC words we looked at can also do a lot more than we used them for. Here are some ideas on other books that can help you learn more about BASIC.

A good source of information is the reference book on BASIC that came with your computer when you bought it. Have you looked at it?

Some people don't know that there are many books about computers at the local bookstore or at the library. Here are some reference books that you can probably find at your local library or bookstore. They go into even more detail than this book.

> *QBASIC by Example*, by Greg Perry (Que, 1992)
>
> *The First Book of GWBASIC*, by Saul Aguiar (SAMS, 1990)
>
> *The Waite Group's GWBASIC Primer Plus*, by D.R. Mackenroth (SAMS, 1991)
>
> *The Waite Group's QBASIC Primer Plus*, by D.R. Mackenroth (SAMS, 1991)
>
> *Using QBASIC*, by Phil Feldman and Tom Rugg (Que, 1991)

Start a Club

You and your friends could even start a BASIC club. You could all work on a large project, but break it down to work on smaller sections. You can also help each other with problems. You might need help setting up a club. Ask a parent or teacher at your school to help you find a meeting place and time. The PTA or PTO could probably help you organize your meetings and find a teacher who knows BASIC.

Most cities have computer user groups. They meet once each month to talk about—what else?—computers! A user group may invite experts to talk about the neat new programs for computers. You can also learn about new computer equipment and products.

Computer Bulletin Boards

Have you ever heard about computer bulletin boards? In the ways they're used, they're kind of like the bulletin boards you see in classrooms, libraries, and stores. Instead of being made of wood and cork, a computer bulletin board uses a computer to keep track of messages.

You need a telephone line and a **modem** (a device that lets your computer make phone calls) to hook your computer to a bulletin board. You might need help from a teacher or your parents to show you how.

Make sure you get permission from your parents before you call a computer bulletin board, because there may be a cost for signing up or using the board.

Once you know how to use the computer bulletin board, you can share ideas about BASIC programming with other people around the world. You can copy some of the BASIC programs that other people have made and use them on your computer. Then you can see how other people solved programming problems, and get new ideas to try yourself.

Good Luck!

We'd love to hear about the programs you build after reading this book. Write and tell us all about them!

Alpha Kids Books
"Building with BASIC"
11711 North College Avenue
Carmel, IN 46032

WORDS, WORDS, WORDS

Here is a list of the new words we talked about in this book. The words are in alphabetical order. Right after this list, you'll find a list of the BASIC commands we talked about in the book.

animation   Programming a picture to look as though it is moving. You can add color and even move your pictures around the screen.

application   A use for a computer program. The job a program is meant to do.

array   A "super variable." A regular variable can only hold one piece of information. An array can hold long lists. Each piece of information is called an element.

ASCII   Short for American Standard Code for Information Interchange. This is a set of codes that BASIC can use to make pictures.

bag of tricks   Your own collection of subroutine programs. You can use these in other programs whenever you need them.

branching   When the program jumps to another section of the computer program.

computer program   A set of instructions that can be understood by a computer. These instruction must be clear and in the proper order, or sequence.

computer programmer   A person who can translate English-language instructions into a high-level computer language.

computer programming language   A computer program that can translate instructions into machine language for the computer.

element   One piece of information in a list or array. The number for that element goes in ( ) after the array name, like this: MESSAGE$ (15) is the fifteenth element in the array called MESSAGE$.

error trapping   Catching player mistakes in the program before they can mess up the program.

flowchart   A map of what the program is supposed to do.

line number   Used by the computer to put the instructions in the right order. (QBASIC does not need line numbers.)

loop   A group of instructions that repeat over and over.

machine language   A special language that all computers understand but very few people do. Your BASIC software translates your programming lines into machine language, and the machine language tells the computer what to do.

organized computer programs   Are easier to make and easier to change than messy programs. Your programs will be more organized if you follow these tips:

1. Have a main part that uses GOSUB to send the work to subroutines.

2. Break big jobs down into smaller subroutines.

pixel   One of the tiny dots on a computer screen.

program list   Lines of instructions for a program. Those lines will have commands and codes that tell a computer what to do.

randomize   To mix up a group of things so that they are in no special order.

spaghetti code   A disorganized, messy program.

statement   Another name for a line of computer instructions.

user-friendly   A type of program that is easy to understand and use.

variable   A storage place for information used by the program. Think of a variable as a storage bin for numbers or messages.

variable names   There are several rules you must follow in naming those little storage bins. If you put a % at the end, it means it is a number. If you put $, it means it is a message of some kind, not a number.

BASIC Commands

CIRCLE

Tells the computer to draw circles and curves.

How You Use It

CIRCLE (x,y), radius, *color*, *start*, *end*, *stretch*

Color, *start*, *end*, and *stretch* are optional—you can choose what to make them.

x,y   The pixel where the center of the circle is located.

radius   The distance from the center to the edge of the circle.

color   A number that tells what color the circle will be.

start   The place to start drawing the circle in a counterclockwise direction.

end   The point at which to stop drawing the circle.

stretch   The number that stretches the circle into an oval.

Example

If you want to draw an oval in the center of the screen, use this CIRCLE statement:

```
10 CIRCLE (160,100),6,,,,2
```

CLS

Clears the computer screen.

How You Use It

```
CLS
```

Example

```
20 CLS
```

COLOR

Picks a color for the computer screen.

How You Use It

```
COLOR x
```

The letter *x* shows where to put the number of a color code.

Example

```
100 COLOR 2
```

DATA

Used to hold information in a program that will be read by a READ command.

How You Use It

```
DATA information
```

or

```
DATA information,information
back
```

information Any piece of information in the list you will be making.

Example

```
10 DATA Mrs.Smith,Mr.Lane,Bobby
```

or

```
20 DATA 0,10,2,30
```

DIM

This tells the maximum number of items that can be in an array.

How You Use It

```
DIM array(x)
```

array is the name of the array you are setting up.

x is the maximum number of items in your list.

Place the DIM statement near the beginning of your program.

Example

You want to create an array called MOVIES$. You know that there will probably be 30 or 40 names in the list. Since you may want to add some names later, you decide to make the list hold 80 names. This is how you would do it:

```
DIM MOVIES$(80)
```

DRAW

Draws figures on the screen.

How You Use It

```
DRAW "draw command"
```

draw command Use the DRAW commands.

Example

Draw a triangle (listed in Chapter 8):

```
DRAW "F60 L120 E60"
```

EDIT (Regular BASIC Only)

Lets you make changes to the program lines.

How You Use It

```
EDIT line number
```

line number The number of the line you want to change in the BASIC program.

Example

If you want to change line number 50 in a program, type this:

```
EDIT 50
```

The line numbered 50 prints on the screen. Move the cursor to the place you want to change. Type right over whatever is on the screen—or press the Insert key if you want the words to scoot to the right as you type.

FILES (Regular BASIC Only)

Lists all the program names.

How You Use It

```
FILES "filenames"
```

filenames The names of the files you want to see on the list. If you don't use this, BASIC will show you all the files on a disk.

Example

If you want to list all the BASIC programs on a disk in the B: drive, type this:

```
FILES "B:*.BAS"
```

FOR and NEXT

Used to repeat program lines over and over.

How You Use It

```
FOR variable = start TO end
     Instruction
NEXT variable
```

Example

You want to print the message "Hip hip hooray!" three times on the computer screen. Type this:

```
1 FOR SHOUT = 1 TO 3
2     PRINT "Hip hip hooray!"
3 NEXT SHOUT
```

GET

Stores a snapshot of a picture from the screen in an array. We used GET to make a picture move across the screen.

How You Use It

```
GET (upper left corner) -
(lower right corner), array
name
```

upper left corner The (x,y) location of the upper left corner of a rectangle. The rectangle should include the picture you want to animate.

lower right corner The (x,y) location of the lower right corner of the rectangle that holds the picture.

array name A name for the picture.

Example

```
GET (10,20) (30,40), DOG
```

This is the GET statement you would use if you had a picture of a dog on your screen, and you wanted to put it into an array called DOG. You could then use a set of PUT statements to move the picture across the screen.

GOSUB

Tells the computer to branch to a subroutine that starts with a certain line number.

How You Use It

```
GOSUB line number
```

Example

```
GOSUB 3200
```

GOTO

Tells the computer to branch to another section of the program.

How You Use It

In regular BASIC or QBASIC, GOTO can look like this:

```
GOTO line number
```

In QBASIC, you can use a label instead of line number. Now GOTO can look like this:

```
GOTO label:
```

Example

If you want the program to branch to the line number 3200, type this:

```
GOTO 3200
```

IF and THEN

Lets the program test variables and do certain instructions if the test is true.

How You Use It

```
IF test THEN do this
```

test Some kind of comparison or condition that the computer checks.

do this What the computer will do if the test is true. If the test is not true, the program ignores the THEN.

Example

Let's say you want the computer to see if the player wants to quit playing the game. The player has already entered a choice, which is either a Y or N. The player entered a Y to play again or a N to quit. Now the program will check the player's answer. Type this:

```
20 IF CHOICE$ = "Y" THEN
GOTO 100
30 IF CHOICE$ = "N" THEN
GOTO 9999
```

INPUT

Tells the computer to wait until the player presses some keys followed by the Enter key.

How You Use It

```
INPUT variable
```

Example

You want the player to enter the player's name. Call the variable FirstName$. Type this:

```
10 INPUT FirstName$
```

LIST (Regular BASIC Only)

Prints the program lines on your computer screen.

How You Use It

        LIST *line number*

line number   The line numbers in a BASIC program.

Example

You want to look at the first few lines of a program so you can remember its name and what it does. The program is currently in your computer's memory. Type this:

        LIST 1-100

or

        LIST -100

If the lines go too fast across the screen, press the Pause key.

LLIST (Regular BASIC Only)

This command works the same as LIST, but it prints the program lines on your printer.

How You Use It

        LLIST *line numbers*

LOAD (Regular BASIC Only)

Loads a file into the current memory or work space. You must LOAD a file before you can LIST or RUN it.

How You Use It

        LOAD "*program name*"

program name   The name of the program you want to use.

Example

If you want to load a program called FORTUNE.BAS from the disk in drive B:, type this:

        LOAD "B:FORTUNE"

or

        LOAD "B:FORTUNE.BAS"

LOCATE

Moves the cursor to a certain pixel on the screen.

How You Use It

        LOCATE *row, column*

Example

You want to print a message on the 12th row down the screen, 15 columns over. Type this:

        30 LOCATE 12,15

NEW (Regular BASIC Only)

Clears out the current memory. Be sure you save the old program if you want to keep it; otherwise, it's gone.

How You Use It

```
NEW
```

Example

You have already saved the current program, and now you want to look at another program. Type this:

```
NEW
```

(QBASIC lets you pick NEW from a pull-down File menu. Regular BASIC lets you type in the word NEW and press Enter.)

ON PLAY

Tells the computer to play the music in a subroutine while the program continues.

How You Use It

```
ON PLAY (x) GOSUB subroutine
```

The program branches to the music subroutine when the number of notes left in the special area of the computer's memory is less than x.

Example

```
ON PLAY (5) GOSUB 4000
```

When five notes are left in the background music, branch to the subroutine that starts on line number 4000—where the music starts over.

PLAY

Tells the computer to play whatever musical notes are in quotation marks.

How You Use It

```
PLAY "musical commands"
```

musical commands are special symbols for musical notes, pauses, and length of notes.

Example

You want the computer to play the sounds Do Re Mi. Type this:

```
=PLAY "C D E"
```

PRINT

Prints on the computer screen any message between quotation marks.

How You Use It

```
PRINT "message"
```

Example

You want to print a message that says "good morning" to the player. The player's name is in a variable called FirstName$. Type this:

```
10 PRINT "Good morning,
",FirstName$
```

PSET

Colors a pixel.

How You Use It

```
PSET (xy point),color
```

xy point   Means the (x,y) location of a pixel.

color   Means the code number for a color.

Example

You want to draw a dot on the screen. Type this:

```
PSET (50,65),3
```

PUT

Draws a picture on the computer screen. The picture must be one that was stored with the GET statement. When the picture is PUT a second time in the same place, it erases the image.

How You Use It

```
PUT (upper left x,y), array
name
```

upper left x,y   A pixel located on the upper left corner of a rectangle where the snapshot in the GET statement will be placed.

array name   The name of the array that holds the snapshot.

Example

You want a picture of the dog to be placed on the screen starting with the upper left corner of the picture on the pixel at (10,15). The name of the array with the picture is DOG. Type this:

```
20 PUT (10,15),DOG
```

READ

Used to put the information from a DATA statement into an element of an array.

How You Use It

```
READ variable name,variable
name,variable name. .
```

Example

You want the next name of the list of your favorite movie stars to be element number 3 in an array called STAR$. Type this:

```
READ STAR$(3)
```

RND

A BASIC command that gives a random number. It picks a number between 0 and 1.

How You Use It

```
RND math formula
```

Example

If the computer picks a random number less than .5, branch to an elephant adventure subroutine at line number 500:

```
IF RND < .5 THEN GOTO 5000
```

RUN

Starts the program.

How You Use It

```
RUN
```

Example

You want to play a computer adventure game. The game program is already in your computer's current memory. Type this:

```
RUN
```

then press Enter or press the F2 key.

(QBASIC users should use the pull-down RUN menu, or press the Shift and F5 key for a shortcut.)

SAVE (Regular BASIC Only)

Stores a copy of the current program on the current disk.

How You Use It

```
SAVE"program name"
```

program name What you want to call the program. If the same name is already in your computer, the program you are saving will erase the old version.

Example

You have corrected a spelling error on your current program called FUNGAME.BAS. You are ready to stop playing with your computer so you can go to baseball practice. You should type this:

```
SAVE"FUNGAME"
```

(QBASIC users should use the pull-down File menu, and highlight SAV(E).

SCREEN

Sets up the screen mode for the computer screen.

How You Use It

```
SCREEN type number
```

type number A 1, 2, or 3, depending on what you want to print on the screen. You can find out what these mean in Chapter 7.

Example

You want to make a picture, using the screen type that puts pixels in 320 columns and 200 rows. Type this:

```
50 SCREEN 1
```

TAB

Moves the cursor 5 spaces each time.

How You Use It

        TAB (*x*)

x   The number of times to move the cursor
5 spaces across a line on the computer
screen.

Example

You want the word "HI" to print on the
screen 15 spaces from the left, so type this:

        PRINT TAB(3);"HI"

APPENDIX B
COOL SYMBOLS

There are many different kinds of computers in the world. There are many different computer program languages that people use to tell those computers what to do.

A long time ago, it was very confusing for computer programmers to write programs that would work on all the different computers in the world. Computer experts agreed among themselves to use one set of symbols that all computers in the whole world can understand.

That set of symbols is called the **ASCII** character set. ASCII stands for American Standard Code for Information Interchange.

Each symbol in the ASCII character set has a special number. The experts all agreed that these characters would always stay the same. No matter what computer (or computer language) uses them, if they are ASCII characters, they are always the same symbol.

Some of those symbols are fun to print out on the computer screen. The way to get them on the screen is to use a PRINT statement, like this:

```
0010 PRINT CHR$(You put the ASCII number in here)
```

BASIC has a function called CHR$($x$) that looks up the number in parentheses in the ASCII character set—and gives you that symbol. Use the CHR$($x$) function with a PRINT statement to print any ASCII symbol.

Try This!

Here is a routine that will show you all the ASCII codes
on your screen

```
1 CLS
2 FOR X = 1 to 256
4   PRINT CHR$(x)       'Prints all the ASCII codes
5 NEXT X
```

Here is a list of symbols you can use in your programs.

Use the symbol's code number in place of the *x* in the CHR$(*x*) function.

Faces

Code	Symbol
1	☺
2	☻

Deck of Playing Card Suits

Code	Symbol
3	♥
4	♦
5	♣
6	♠

Funny Symbols

Code	Symbol
7	●
8	▮
15	—
22	-
219	█
220	▄
221	▌
222	▐
223	▀

Greek Symbols

Code	Symbol
224	α
225	β
226	Γ
227	π
228	Σ
229	σ
230	μ
231	τ
232	Φ
233	Θ
234	Ω
235	d
236	∞
237	φ
238	ε

Funny Patterns

Code	Symbol
176	▓
177	▓
178	▓

Male and Female

Code	Symbol
11	♂
12	♀

Musical Notes

Code	Symbol
13	♪
14	♪

Arrows

Code	Symbol
16	▶
17	◀
18	↕
23	↕
24	↑
25	↓
26	→
27	←
29	↔
30	▲
31	▼

Funny Lines

Code	Symbol
179	│
180	┤
181	╡
182	╢
183	╖
184	╕
185	╣
186	║
187	╗
188	╝
189	╜
190	╛
191	┐
192	╟
193	┴
194	┬
195	├
196	─
197	┼
198	

Funny Lines (continued)

Code	Symbol
199	╞
200	╚
201	╔
202	╩
203	╦
204	╠
205	═
206	╬
207	╧
208	╨
209	╤
210	╥
211	╙
212	╘
213	╒
214	╓
215	╫
216	╪
217	┘
218	┌

CREATE YOUR OWN ADVENTURE

You'll have fun making up an adventure story for your computer game. This section tells you how to set up your adventure story so you can turn it into a BASIC computer program. Here are some of the parts that go into writing a good story:

- Plot
- Setting
- Characters
- Scenario

Your computer game will be better if you spend a lot of time planning the story before you begin putting the program on the computer. You'll have fewer errors, and you won't leave out important parts of the story.

What Is an Interactive Adventure Game?

A **game** has a player, and it should be fun. **Adventure** means that something happens to that player, perhaps a surprise. **Interactive** means that the players seem to "talk" to the computer when they make choices. Each choice changes the way the adventure will end up.

Have you ever played an adventure game? There are several popular games, such as the Carmen Sandiego or Super Solvers game series, Hero's Quest, and many others. Have you ever wondered how those work? After you finish reading this book, you will have a better idea.

Do you know what makes a good game? Let's start with an interesting adventure story.

Plot

The plot is the plan of action in the adventure. The plot tells what happens and to whom. An interesting plot could include secret schemes of the characters. The story can include several plots, leading the player into different directions.

A plot could include:

- Chasing clues.

- Winding through secret tunnels.

- Visiting different cities.

Your plot needs some kind of goal. The goal might be to complete a mission and come out alive. The goal could be to find a treasure or a clue to solve a mystery.

Your plot can twist and turn. You should make up several small adventures. When more adventures happen to your player, the game will last longer.

Setting

The **setting** of the adventure story includes these things:

- Time (year, month, clock time).

- Place.

- Mood (how you would feel in this time or place).

Here are some ideas to get you started. Your story could take place in:

- Prehistoric North America.

- The year 4400 A.D. on a distant planet.

- A crowded mall during the holiday shopping season.

You can use a fantasy setting, or your setting can be realistic.

Try This!

Let's get the cobwebs out of your head! Grab a sheet of notebook paper. Think up some settings you might want to use in your adventure story. Write them all down, even if they seem crazy right now. Use your imagination. Keep your list handy.

Characters

What sort of characters will your player meet? The characters do not even have to be human. Your characters could be:

- Animals
- Shape-changing aliens
- Objects which seem alive, such as a talking TV or computer, a rock, trees, or clouds

Your imagination has no limits in this application.

Your story will come alive through the personalities of the characters. Will your characters have any of these traits?

- Good, reliable, trustworthy
- Evil, diabolic, wicked
- Intelligent
- Bashful
- Bold, courageous

Try This!

Grab your notebook again. Turn to a new page. Start your own list of characters that you might want to include. Figure out how they look and how they act and write that down, too.

Scenario—Combine Plot and Setting

So far you have written down a few ideas about some characters, setting, and plot. Next you'll put them together to set up a **scenario** for the adventure. A good scenario describes the story in a way that gives you a mental picture.

Your scenario should get your player into the adventure right away to make the game fun from the beginning. Make sure you add some kind of obstacle in the adventure to make the game more challenging. Will your player find:

- A ravine full of snakes?
- An important clue in a locked trunk?
- A castle moat?

Will your story be funny or serious? Will it be friendly or hostile? You can put emotions into the story, just by the way you write it.

Here is a sample scenario:

> *You are traveling through the English countryside 600 years ago. You cross a river and climb to the top of a hill. In the distance, you see a large stone building.*
>
> *There is a stone wall about 30 feet high and 12 feet thick running all around it. On top of the wall there are several round towers with narrow windows in them. You look closely and see that there are archers with bows and arrows aimed at the enemy outside the wall.*

You must figure out a way to get the important message you are carrying to the master of the castle. But you cannot be captured by the enemy outside the walls. And, you must avoid being shot by the archers behind the walls of the castle . . . .

Your scenario can include information you study at school. This scenario would be a fun way to show what you learned about the Middle Ages. If you make the scenario realistic, your game teaches the player something new while he enjoys playing the adventure. (Talk about impressing your history teacher!)

Here is another sample scenario:

Your microscopic ship enters the left side of the patient's heart. The pumping power of the heart propels your ship forward into the large artery that carries blood to the rest of the body.

You must now find and capture the invading organisms, and repair the damaged section of the artery. You must work quickly, before the time limit on your mission is up.

You prepare to position the robotic arm of your ship. Bad luck. The arm is jammed. Will you try to fix it from inside the ship, or will you suit up to go outside the ship and fix the jammed piece yourself?

Scientists are studying the idea of using microscopic robots in medicine, but not in order to send tiny people through the body in little ships! This scenario combines truth and fiction to make a good adventure.

Try This!

Grab your notebook again! From your own list of settings, pick your favorite. Start to form a scenario, complete with events and characters. Write down events. You should include a goal and obstacle.

Write down some choices the player will make. Figure out when your player will make these decisions. Figure out the sequence, or order, in which the events will take place.

Let the adventure begin!

Arrange Your Story

Now you need to arrange your story. You can draw a picture of your story, like a map. A picture will help you understand how your story goes together. With a map or drawing by your side, the next step will be to turn the story into BASIC programming code.

Draw a map to organize the events in the right order. Look back to your notes on scenario and characters. Don't be afraid to change things around as you get into drawing the picture.

Your map should use special symbols to show what is happening in the story. We will use these shapes:

○   The beginning or end of the adventure

◇   A decision by the player

▢   A section of the story

Here is a map of the microscopic journey adventure.

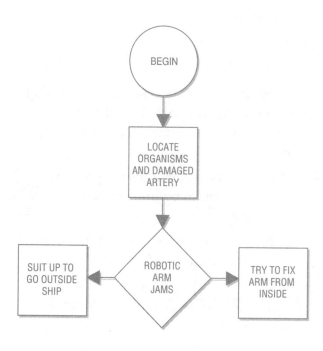

Write the Text

The next step when writing a good adventure game is to write down what you want the player to read as he plays the game. You should use a different notebook page for each event of the adventure. You should write down a label for each section, along with a brief description, such as "Artery," or "Fix Robotic Arm," or "Repair from Inside Ship."

Write down what the characters say to each other. Write down any questions the player will answer when he makes a decision.

Here are some important hints that give your game some polish. (Did you listen to your English teacher when you had this in class?)

- Use correct spelling.
- Use correct punctuation.
- Use colorful descriptions.

Here are some ways to use colorful descriptions:

Boring descriptions	Use these instead
sad	dejected, cheerless, lonely
tall	gangly, towering, lofty
scared	petrified, spooked, terrified
strange	peculiar, curious, bizarre
hungry	famished, ravenous

Try to be creative. Did you think computer programming would be boring? No way!

Keep reading to find out what to do now that you have an organized story.

Assign Line Number Ranges

Each line of a BASIC computer program starts with a line number. The line numbers tell the computer which line to read first. In some ways, the computer reads BASIC programming language like you read English:

- The computer reads the program from top to bottom in line-number order.
- The computer reads each line of the program from left to right.

Tip Offs

Do you have some friends who love to make up wild stories? Get them together for a "thinking" party. Ask them to think up a great adventure. Take notes, and then put it into a computer adventure game.

You don't know yet what all the lines of the program will look like. But you do know some of the sections of the adventure story.

You can assign a **range** of line numbers to each section, starting at the beginning of the adventure story. Each range of line numbers should be large enough for all the lines you have so far. Leave enough room in each section to add more lines to the program later.

Here is an example of line number ranges in the Heart Adventure:

Event	Line Numbers
Introduction	0–99
Prepare Ship's Supplies	100–199
Begin Mission	200–299
Problem with Robotic Arm	300–399
Fix it from Inside?	400–499
Suit up to go Outside Ship?	500–599
Encounter Organisms	600–699
Kill Organisms?	700–799
Capture Organisms Alive?	800–899
Play Again?	900–999

QBASIC Users!

Line numbers are optional in QBASIC. You can add line numbers or leave them out. Instead of using line numbers, think up a **label**, or name, to identify sections of the adventure story. Figure out short names for each of your scenes. Labels can have up to 40 characters and can include numbers and letters.

Event	Label Name
Introduction	*Introduction*
Prepare Ship's Supplies	*PrepareSupplies*
Begin Mission	*BeginMission*
Problem with Robotic Arm	*ProblemArm*
Fix it from Inside?	*InsideFix*
Suit up to go Outside Ship?	*OutsideFix*
Encounter Organisms	*EncounterOrganisms*
Kill Organisms?	*KillOrganisms*
Capture Organisms Alive?	*CaptureOrganisms*
Play Again?	*PlayAgain?*

Summary

This appendix showed you how to make up a good adventure story. You learned about some parts that make up a good story. These parts are:

- Plot
- Setting
- Characters
- Scenario

You also learned how to turn that adventure story into a computer game. To do that, you must:

1. Arrange the story into a picture, or map.

2▸ Give each part of the story a range of line numbers. Those line-number ranges get the story ready for BASIC programming codes.

Congratulations! You finished reading this whole appendix. Your next mission is to think up a totally awesome adventure. After you write your excellent adventure, you can use this book about BASIC to help you turn it into a computer game.

APPENDIX D
PROGRAM LISTINGS

H ere is a listing of all the programs mentioned in this book. I've also included some useful short programs that you can add to your "bag of tricks." All these programs are on the disk that came with this book.

8BALL.BAS

This program simulates an 8-Ball toy. This version only uses words—no graphics.

```
10  REM Program 8BALL.BAS
20  REM Simulates an 8-Ball toy
30  CLS
40  REM There are 20 messages in the 8-Ball
50  DIM MESSAGE$(20)
60  DATA "It is certain"
70  DATA "Signs point to yes"
80  DATA "Outlook good"
90  DATA "My sources say no"
100 DATA "It is decidedly so"
110 DATA "You may rely on it"
120 DATA "Ask again later"
130 DATA "Better not tell you now"
140 DATA "Very doubtful"
150 DATA "Yes, definitely"
160 DATA "Cannot predict now"
170 DATA "My reply is no"
180 DATA "As I see it, yes"
190 DATA "Don't count on it"
200 DATA "Outlook not so good"
210 DATA "Without a doubt"
220 DATA "Really hazy, try again"
230 DATA "Concentrate and ask again"
```

```
240 DATA "Yes"
250 DATA "No"
260 REM Assign a number to each message in the
265 REM array called MESSAGE$
270 FOR COUNT = 1 TO 20
280     READ MESSAGE$(COUNT)
290 NEXT COUNT
300 REM Start game
310 LOCATE 18
320 PRINT "Would you like to ask the all-knowing"
325 PRINT "8-Ball a question?"
330 PRINT "Type in Y for yes, or N for no, then press ENTER"
340 INPUT YESNO$
350 REM Don't let the player enter anything but Y,y,N,n
360 IF YESNO$ = "y" OR YESNO$ = "Y" THEN GOTO 440
370 IF YESNO$ = "n" THEN GOTO 390
380 IF YESNO$ <> "N" THEN 330
390 REM Player doesn't want to play anymore
400 CLS
410 PRINT "Wasn't that fun?"
420 PRINT "See you later"
430 END
440 CLS
450 REM Ask player a question now, then give them a random answer
460 PRINT "Type your question now, then press ENTER to "
470 PRINT "shake up the mystical 8-Ball."
480 INPUT SHAKEITUP$
490 REM Randomly choose the message from the 8-Ball
500 RANDOMIZE TIMER
510 ANSWER = INT(20 * RND(1)) + 1
520 LOCATE 10
530 PRINT "The wise 8-Ball says"
540 PRINT MESSAGE$(ANSWER)
550 REM     Go back to see if player wants to play
555 REM     this silly game again.
560 GOTO 320
```

8BALLPIC.BAS

This makes a picture of an 8-Ball. It's also used as a subroutine in the FORTUNE.BAS program.

```
10000 REM Program 8BALLPIC.BAS draws 8-Ball picture.
10100 GOSUB 10700 'Housekeeping:
10200 GOSUB 11400 'Draw 8-Ball:
10300 GOSUB 12800 'Shake the Ball:
10400 GOSUB 13900 'Turn it over:
10500 GOTO 14700 'End routine:
10600 REM *********sub-routines**************
10700   REM Housekeeping:
10800   KEY OFF
10900   CLS
11000   SCREEN 1
11100   DIM IMAGE(5000)
11200 RETURN
11300 REM ********************************
11400 REM Draw 8-Ball:
11500     CIRCLE (160, 100), 80      'Large circle
11600     CIRCLE (160, 65), 30       'Smaller circle at top
11700     CIRCLE (160, 56), 6        'Top Part of 8
11800     CIRCLE (160, 69), 6        'Bottom of 8
11900     CIRCLE (160, 56), 10       'Top Part of 8
12000     CIRCLE (160, 69), 10       'Bottom of 8
12100     PAINT (140, 75)
12200     PAINT (160, 56)
12300     PAINT (160, 68)
12400 GET (75, 25)-(250, 170), IMAGE           'Take snapshot of ball
12500 CLS
12600 RETURN
12700 REM ***********************************
12800 REM Shake the 8-Ball:
12900   NOW! = TIMER
13000   WHILE TIMER < NOW! + 2 'About 25 seconds
13100   REM The ball seems to move back and forth.
13200       PUT (75, 10), IMAGE
13300       PUT (75, 10), IMAGE
13400       PUT (95, 10), IMAGE
13500       PUT (95, 10), IMAGE
13600   WEND
13700 RETURN
13800 REM ***********************************
13900 REM Turn it over:
```

```
14000    CLS
14100      CIRCLE (160, 100), 130      'Large circle
14200      LINE (50, 80)-(270, 120), , B
14300    LOCATE 12, 8
14400    PRINT "Concentrate and ask again"
14500 RETURN
14600 REM **********************************
14700 REM End routine
14800 END
```

8BALLSUB.BAS

This version of 8BALL is written with subroutines, and is more organized.

```
100 REM Program 8BALLSUB.BAS   'Structured Program
200 REM Simulates an 8-Ball toy
300 GOSUB 1300     'Housekeeping:
400 GOSUB 4200   'Play or not:
500 IF YESNO$ = "N" THEN GOTO 800
600 GOSUB 5400     'Shake 8-Ball:
700 GOTO 400     'Find out if player wants to play again
800 REM Player doesn't want to play anymore
900 CLS
1000 PRINT "Wasn't that fun?"
1100 PRINT "See you later"
1200 END
1300 REM Housekeeping:**************************
1400    CLS
1500    REM There are 20 messages in the 8-Ball
1600    DIM MESSAGE$(20)
1700    DATA "It is certain"
1800    DATA "Signs point to yes"
1900    DATA "Outlook good"
2000    DATA " My sources say no"
2100    DATA "It is decidedly so"
2200    DATA "You may rely on it"
2300    DATA "Ask again later"
2400    DATA "Better not tell you now"
2500    DATA "Very doubtful"
2600    DATA "Yes, definitely"
2700    DATA "Cannot predict now"
2800    DATA "My reply is no"
2900    DATA "As I see it, yes"
```

continues

```
3000    DATA "Don't count on it"
3100    DATA "Outlook not so good"
3200    DATA "Without a doubt"
3300    DATA "Really hazy, try again"
3400    DATA "Concentrate and ask again"
3500    DATA "Yes"
3600    DATA "No"
3700    REM assign a number to each message in the array called
        MESSAGE$
3800    FOR COUNT = 1 TO 20
3900       READ MESSAGE$(COUNT)
4000    NEXT COUNT
4100 RETURN     ' return to Main part of program
4200 REM Play or not:*******************************
4300 REM Asks the player whether (s)he wants to play or not
4400    LOCATE 23
4500    PRINT "Would you like to ask the all-knowing 8-Ball a
        question?"
4600    PRINT "Type in Y for yes, or N to end game, then press
        ENTER"
4700    INPUT YESNO$
4800    REM Don't let the player enter anything but Y,y,N,n
4900    PRINT "Your answer is "; YESNO$
5000      IF YESNO$ = "y" OR YESNO$ = "Y" THEN YESNO$ = "Y"
5100      IF YESNO$ = "n" OR YESNO$ = "N" THEN YESNO$ = "N"
5200      IF YESNO$ <> "Y" AND YESNO$ <> "N" THEN GOTO 4600 'Player
        error
5300 RETURN
5400 REM Shake 8-Ball****************
5500    GOSUB 5900 ' Type question
5600    GOSUB 6500 ' Random pick
5700 GOSUB 6900    ' Print answer
5800 RETURN
5900 REM Type question:   **********************
6000    CLS
6100    PRINT "Type your question now, then press ENTER to"
6200    PRINT "shake up the mystical 8-Ball."
6300    INPUT SHAKEITUP$
6400 RETURN
6500 REM Random pick*************************************
6600    RANDOMIZE TIMER
6700    ANSWER = INT(20 * RND(1)) + 1
6800 RETURN
6900 REM Print answer *****************************
```

```
7000    LOCATE 10
7100    PRINT "The wise 8-Ball says"
7200    PRINT MESSAGE$(ANSWER)
7300 RETURN
```

ALPHABET.BAS

This program plays "The Alphabet Song" in two versions—one with notes the same length,
and the other with notes the proper length.

```
5   REM ALPHABET.BAS Shows the length of notes
10 PLAY "C C G G A A G F F E E D D D D C"
15 REM These notes have different lengths
20 PLAY "L2 C C G G A A L1G L2 F F E E L4D D D D L1C"
```

ANIMOCTI.BAS

This program animates the octopus drawn in OCTCOLOR.BAS.

```
100   REM Program: ANIMOCTI.BAS (Demonstrates SCREEN 1 statement)
200   REM Modified for screen 1; shows color, animation, circles
300   GOSUB 1000              'Housekeeping
400   GOSUB 3400              'Draw octopus
500   GOSUB 1700              'Background
600   GOSUB 7300              'Animate octopus
700   GOTO 10800              'End routine
800   REM ****subroutines******
900   REM
1000 REM Housekeeping:
1100 DIM IMAGE(8000)          'Dimension storage array
1200 KEY OFF
1300 SCREEN 1                 'Select GRAPHICS
1400 COLOR 3                  'Background color of ocean
1500 CLS
1600 RETURN
1700 REM *********************************************
1800 REM Background:
1900 REM Wave A
2000 FOR WAVE = 250 TO 300 STEP 25
2100    CIRCLE (WAVE, 20), 12, 1, PI, 0, .5
2200 NEXT WAVE
2300 REM Wave B
```

continues

```
2400 FOR WAVE = 250 TO 300 STEP 25
2500 CIRCLE (WAVE, 150), 12, 1, PI, 0, .5
2600 NEXT WAVE
2700 REM Wave C
2800 FOR WAVE = 25 TO 75 STEP 25
2900     CIRCLE (WAVE, 120), 12, 1, PI, 0, .5
3000 NEXT WAVE
3100 REM LINE (100, 90)-STEP(20, 20), 3, B
3200 REM LINE (150, 90)-STEP(20, 20), 2, BF
3300 RETURN
3400 REM *********************************************
3500 REM Draw octopus:
3600         PI = 4 * ATN(1) 'Calculate value of Pi
3700 REM Outline of Head
3800         CIRCLE (150, 60), 60, , 10 * PI / 6, 8 * PI / 6, 2
3900 REM Eyes
4000         CIRCLE (155, 95), 5
4100         CIRCLE (145, 95), 5
4200 REM Arms
4300 REM Each arm needs two partial circles
4400 REM BOTTOM ARM ON RIGHT
4500         CIRCLE (170, 125), 12, , PI / 2, 3 * PI / 2, 1
4600         CIRCLE (170, 150), 12, , 3 * PI / 2, PI / 2, 1
4700 REM BOTTOM ARM ON LEFT
4800         CIRCLE (145, 125), 12, , PI / 2, 3 * PI / 2, 1
4900         CIRCLE (145, 150), 12, , 3 * PI / 2, PI / 2, 1
5000 REM ARM ON RIGHT STRAIGHT OUT
5100         CIRCLE (200, 100), 12, , 0, PI
5200         CIRCLE (224, 100), 12, , PI, 0
5300 REM ARM ON LEFT STRAIGHT OUT
5400         CIRCLE (100, 100), 12, , 0, PI
5500         CIRCLE (76, 100), 12, , PI, 0
5600 REM ARM ON RIGHT TOP
5700         CIRCLE (200, 75), 12, , PI / 6, PI
5800         CIRCLE (217, 60), 12, , 2.5 * PI / 2, PI / 6
5900 REM ARM ON LEFT TOP
6000         CIRCLE (100, 75), 12, , 0, 5 * PI / 6
6100         CIRCLE (83, 60), 12, , 5 * PI / 6, 1.75 * PI
6200 REM ARM ANGLED DOWN AND RIGHT
6300         CIRCLE (175, 120), 20, , 11 * PI / 6, PI / 2, .6
6400         CIRCLE (203, 135), 15, , 4 * PI / 6, 1.75 * PI, 1
6500 REM ARM ANGLED DOWN AND LEFT
6600         CIRCLE (115, 120), 20, , PI / 3, 7 * PI / 6, .6
6700         CIRCLE (93, 133), 12, , 7 * PI / 6, PI / 3, .6
```

```
6800 GOSUB 9800                           'Eyebrows
6900 GET (50, 0)-(240, 175), IMAGE        'Store snapshot in Image
7000 CLS
7100 RETURN
7200 REM ***************************************************
7300 REM   Animate octopus:
7400 GOSUB 7900                 'GO FORWARD
7500 GOSUB 8400                 'GO BACKWARD
7600 PUT (X, 0), IMAGE
7700 RETURN
7800 REM ***************************************************
7900 REM Go forward:
8000     FOR X = 25 TO 100 STEP 5
8100         GOSUB 9000             'GOSUB Go octopus
8200     NEXT X
8300 RETURN
8400 REM ***************************************************
8500 REM Go backward:
8600   FOR X = 100 TO 25 STEP -5
8700     GOSUB 9000               'GOSUB Go octopus
8800     NEXT X
8900 RETURN
9000 REM   ***************************************************
9100 REM Go octopus:
9200         PUT (X, 0), IMAGE
9300           NOW! = TIMER                'Pause the action
9400           WHILE TIMER > NOW! + .15    'for .15 second
9500           WEND
9600         PUT (X, 0), IMAGE
9700 RETURN
9800 REM ***************************************************
9900 REM Eyebrows:
10000 REM Angry
10100 REM PSET (150, 92)                'Position for next DRAW
          statements
10200 REM DRAW "BE5 E5 BG10 BH5 H5"   'Angry
10300 REM    'Shy
10400     PSET (150, 65)                'Position for next DRAW
          statements
10500     DRAW "BF5 F5 BH10 BG5 G5"   'Shy
10600     PRESET (150, 65)             'Hide the point
10700 RETURN
10800 REM End routine *****************************************
10900 END
```

BABY.BAS

This program draws four baby faces. It shows how to use circles and lines to draw pictures.

```
100 REM Program: BABY.BAS (Demonstrates CIRCLE statements)
200 GOSUB 1000 'Housekeeping
300 GOSUB 1500 'Happy baby
400 GOSUB 2900 'Shouting baby
500 GOSUB 4800 'Shy baby
600 GOSUB 6500 'Singing baby
700 GOSUB 7600 'Print labels
800 GOTO 8000  'End routine
900 REM*** SUBROUTINES ****************************
1000 REM Housekeeping:
1100     SCREEN 2 'Select high-resolution graphics
1200     KEY OFF
1300     PI = 4 * ATN(1)
1400 RETURN
1500 REM Happy baby: ****************************
1600     CIRCLE (100, 48), 100                    'Head
1700 REM Eyes
1800     CIRCLE (60, 40), 20, , PI / 4, .75 * PI   'Left Eye
1900     CIRCLE (140, 40), 20, , PI / 4, .75 * PI  'Right Eye
2000 REM Hair
2100     CIRCLE (60, 15), 40, , PI / 20, .6 * PI
2200 REM Nose
2300     CIRCLE (100, 40), 10, , PI / 4, .75 * PI
2400 REM Mouth
2500     CIRCLE (100, 60), 40, , -PI, -.001 * PI
2600     DRAW "BG5"  'Move LPR inside of baby's mouth
2700     DRAW "P1,2" 'Color baby's mouth
2800 RETURN
2900 REM Shouting baby: **************************
3000     CIRCLE (500, 48), 100                    'Head
3100 REM Left Eye and Eyebrow
3200     CIRCLE (430, 40), 2                      'Left Eye
3300     DRAW "TA-30"                             'Left Eyebrow
3400     DRAW "BU10 R10 L20"
3500 REM Right Eye and Eyebrow
3600     CIRCLE (510, 40), 2                      'Right Eye
3700     DRAW "TA 30"                             'Right Eyebrow
3800     DRAW "BU10 R10 L20"
3900 REM Hair
4000     CIRCLE (430, 15), 40, , PI / 20, .6 * PI
4100 REM Nose
```

```
4200      CIRCLE (470, 50), 10, , PI / 4, .75 * PI
4300 REM Mouth
4400      CIRCLE (470, 75), 35, , -11 * PI / 6, -5 * PI / 6
4500      DRAW "BE5"   'Move LPR inside of baby's mouth
4600      DRAW "P1,2" 'Color baby's mouth
4700 RETURN
4800 REM Shy baby:  ***********************
4900      CIRCLE (100, 148), 100                    'Head
5000 REM Left Eyes and Eyebrows
5100      CIRCLE (70, 140), 2                     'Left Eye
5200      DRAW "TA50"                             'Left Eyebrow
5300      DRAW "BU10 R10 L20"
5400 REM Right Eyes and Eyebrows
5500      CIRCLE (130, 140), 2
5600      DRAW "TA-50"                             'Left Eyebrow
5700      DRAW "BU10 R10 L20"
5800 REM Hair
5900      CIRCLE (60, 115), 40, , PI / 20, .6 * PI
6000 REM Nose
6100 REM CIRCLE (100, 160), 20, , PI / 4, .75 * PI
6200 REM Mouth
6300      CIRCLE (100, 160), 30, , PI, .001 * PI, .2
6400 RETURN
6500 REM Singing baby: ***************************
6600      CIRCLE (500, 148), 100                   'Head
6700 REM Mouth
6800      CIRCLE (500, 140), 20, , , , .6
6900 REM Eyes
7000  CIRCLE (465, 115), 15, , 8 * PI / 6, 0     'Left Eyebrow
7100  CIRCLE (535, 115), 15, , PI, 10 * PI / 6  'Right Eyebrow
7200 REM Hair
7300      CIRCLE (465, 110), 40, , PI / 20, .6 * PI
7400 REM Nose
7500 RETURN
7600 REM Print labels: ***************************
7700      LOCATE 12, 18: PRINT "Laughing Baby"; TAB(46); "Shouting
          Baby"
7800      LOCATE 23, 25: PRINT "Shy Baby"; TAB(38); "Singing Baby"
7900 RETURN
8000 REM End routine:
8100  END
```

BCKMUSIC.BAS

Here is something to add to your "bag of tricks"—a subroutine that plays background music in any program.

```
20000 REM Program BCKMUSIC.BAS  Adds background music to any
      program
20100 REM    Change Line 21400 for tune, then add as subroutine to
20150 REM    other programs
20200 ON PLAY(5) GOSUB 21300    'Play More Trap when 5 notes are
      left
20300 PLAY ON
20400 PLAY "MB"                 'Turn on Background Music
20500 GOSUB 21300              'Start the tune
20600 SCREEN 1
20700 FOR COUNTER = 1 TO 3000   'Makes a design on screen while you
20800      X = RND * 320        'listen and test music or sound
20900      Y = RND * 200
21000     PSET (X, Y)
21100 NEXT COUNTER
21200 END                       'Change this to RETURN in big
      program
21300 REM PlayMore:             'This line of music will play in
      background
21400     LINE1$ = "L1 N3 L2 N4 P4 L1 N3 L2 N4 P4 L1 N3 L2 N4 P4 L1
      N3 L2 N4"
21500     PLAY LINE1$
21600   RETURN
```

BOY.BAS

This program draws a picture of a boy.

```
100 REM Program: BOY.BAS   Demonstrates CIRCLE statement and
110 REM                    uses a loop to draw hair
120 REM
200 SCREEN 2                    'Select high-resolution graphics
300 CLS
400 REM Head ********************************************
500 PI = 4 * ATN(1)
600 CIRCLE (300, 100), 100, , 5 * PI / 6, PI / 6, .8
700 REM Eyes ********************************************
800 CIRCLE (280, 90), 2        'Left Eye
900 DRAW "BH10 R15 BR27 R15"
```

```
1000 CIRCLE (320, 90), 2        'Right Eye
1100 REM Hair **************************************************
1200 PSET (212, 65)             'Places marker at top left of head
1300 HAIR$ = "NU20 BR5"
1400    FOR MOVE = 1 TO 37
1500       DRAW HAIR$
1600    NEXT MOVE
1700 REM Nose **************************************************
1800 CIRCLE (300, 110), 10, , PI / 4, .75 * PI
1900 REM Mouth *************************************************
2000 CIRCLE (300, 120), 30, , 1.25 * PI, 1.75 * PI, .2
2100 END
```

FORTUNE.BAS

The 8BALL and BALLPIC programs have been combined, with music and a story added.

```
100 REM Program FORTUNE.BAS
200 REM Simulates an 8-Ball toy
300 GOSUB 1300        'Housekeeping
350 GOSUB 20000       'Play music
375 GOSUB 30000       'Gypsy Story
400 GOSUB 4200        'Play or not
500 IF YESNO$ = "N" THEN GOTO 800
600 GOSUB 5400        'Shake 8-Ball:
700 GOTO 400          'Find out if player wants to play again
800 REM Player doesn't want to play anymore
900 CLS
1000 PRINT "Wasn't that fun?"
1100 PRINT "See you later"
1200 END
1300 REM Housekeeping:************************
1400    CLS
1500    REM There are 20 messages in the 8-Ball
1600    DIM MESSAGE$(20)
1700    DATA "It is certain"
1800    DATA "Signs point to yes"
1900    DATA "Outlook good"
2000    DATA " My sources say no"
2100    DATA "It is decidedly so"
2200    DATA "You may rely on it"
2300    DATA "Ask again later"
2400    DATA "Better not tell you now"
```

continues

```
2500    DATA "Very doubtful"
2600    DATA "Yes, definitely"
2700    DATA "Cannot predict now"
2800    DATA "My reply is no"
2900    DATA "As I see it, yes"
3000    DATA "Don't count on it"
3100    DATA "Outlook not so good"
3200    DATA "Without a doubt"
3300    DATA "Really hazy, try again"
3400    DATA "Concentrate, ask again"
3500    DATA "Yes"
3600    DATA "No"
3700 REM Assign a number to each message in the array called
     MESSAGE$
3800    FOR COUNT = 1 TO 20
3900        READ MESSAGE$(COUNT)
4000    NEXT COUNT
4100 RETURN              'Return to Main part of program
4200 REM Play or not ********************************
4300 REM Asks the player whether (s)he wants to play or not
4400    LOCATE 21
4500    PRINT "Would you like to ask the all knowing 8-Ball a
        question?"
4600    PRINT "Type in Y for yes, or N to end game, then press
        ENTER"
4700    INPUT YESNO$
4800    REM Don't let the player enter anything but Y,y,N,n
4900    PRINT "Your answer is "; YESNO$
5000      IF YESNO$ = "y" OR YESNO$ = "Y" THEN YESNO$ = "Y"
5100      IF YESNO$ = "n" OR YESNO$ = "N" THEN YESNO$ = "N"
5200      IF YESNO$ <> "Y" AND YESNO$ <> "N" THEN GOTO 4600 'Player
        error
5300 RETURN
5400 REM Shake 8-Ball *****************
5500    GOSUB 5900        'Type Question
5600    GOSUB 6500        'Random Pick
5650    GOSUB 10000       '8-Ball Picture
5700    GOSUB 6900        'Print Answer
5800 RETURN
5900 REM Type question **********************
6000    CLS
6100    PRINT "Type your question now, then press ENTER to"
```

```
6200    PRINT "shake up the mystical 8-Ball."
6300    INPUT SHAKEITUP$
6400 RETURN
6500 REM Random pick ********************************
6600    RANDOMIZE TIMER
6700    ANSWER = INT(20 * RND(1)) + 1
6800 RETURN
6900 REM Print answer ******************************
7000    LOCATE 14, 10
7200    PRINT MESSAGE$(ANSWER)
7300 RETURN
10000 REM  8-Ball picture ****************************
10100 GOSUB 10700 'Housekeeping:
10200 GOSUB 11400 'Draw 8-Ball:
10300 GOSUB 12800 'Shake the 8-Ball:
10400 GOSUB 13900 'Turn it over:
10500 RETURN
10600 REM *********sub-routines**************
10700    REM Housekeeping:
10800    KEY OFF
10900    CLS
11000    SCREEN 1
11100    DIM IMAGE(5000)
11200 RETURN
11300 REM ********************************
11400 REM Draw 8-Ball
11500    CIRCLE (160, 100), 80          'Large circle
11600    CIRCLE (160, 65), 30           'Smaller circle at top
11700    CIRCLE (160, 56), 6            'Top Part of 8
11800    CIRCLE (160, 69), 6            'Bottom of 8
11900    CIRCLE (160, 56), 10           'Top Part of 8
12000    CIRCLE (160, 69), 10           'Bottom of 8
12100    PAINT (140, 75)
12200    PAINT (160, 56)
12300    PAINT (160, 68)
12400 GET (75, 25)-(250, 170), IMAGE   'Take snapshot of ball
12500 CLS
12600 RETURN
12700 REM ********************************
12800 REM Shake the 8-Ball:
12900    NOW! = TIMER
13000    WHILE TIMER < NOW! + 2          'About 25 seconds
13100    REM The ball seems to move back and forth
13200        PUT (75, 10), IMAGE
```

```
13300        PUT (75, 10), IMAGE
13400        PUT (95, 10), IMAGE
13500        PUT (95, 10), IMAGE
13600    WEND
13700 RETURN
13800 REM **********************************
13900 REM Turn it over:
14000    CLS
14100        CIRCLE (147, 100), 91              'Large circle
14200        LINE (63, 90)-(230, 120), , B
14500 RETURN
20000 REM Gypsy Tune:********************************
20050 REM Play Gypsy Dance (by G. Verdi)
20100 REM
20200 ON PLAY(5) GOSUB 21300  'Play More trap when 5 notes are left
20300 PLAY ON
20400 PLAY "MB"                       'Turn on Background Music
20500 GOSUB 21300                     'Start the tune on line 21300
20700 REM FOR COUNTER = 1 TO 15000   'The next few lines are now
      remarks
20800 REM     X = RND * 320          'because they are used only for
      testing.
20900 REM     Y = RND * 200          'They draw dots on screen while
      you test
21000 REM     PSET (X, Y)            'the song.
21100 REM NEXT COUNTER
21200 RETURN
21300 REM Play More: This line of music will play in background
21400    LINE1$ = " O4 E C E C <L2A. L4 A B > C D < B A A A P4 > "
21500    PLAY LINE1$
21600   RETURN
30000 REM Gypsy Story:  ****************************************
30100 PRINT "Gypsies dance and sing in the moonlight. You hear the"
30200 PRINT "music of violins and tambourines. A gypsy woman
      wearing"
30300 PRINT "dangling beads and scarves sits at a table nearby."
30400 PRINT
30500 PRINT "As you walk up, she welcomes you to join in for a look
      at"
30600 PRINT "her magic 8-Ball. What will it tell you?"
30700 PRINT "What mysteries unfold on this night?"
30800 RETURN
```

GYPSYTUN.BAS

This program plays "Gypsy Dance," a song which is used in FORTUNE.BAS.

```
10 REM Program GYPSYTUN.BAS          'Gypsy Dance by G. Verdi
20 LINE1$ = "MB O4 E C E C <L2A. L4 A B > C D < B A A A P4 > "
30 LINE2$ = "MB O4 E C E C <L2A. L4 A B > C D < B A A A >A"
40 LINE3$ = "MB O4 G F E D C C A G F E D C C L2E. L4"
50 PLAY LINE1$
60 PLAY LINE2$
70 PLAY LINE3$
80 PLAY LINE1$
90 END
```

INKEY.BAS

A subroutine you can use which tests for any key being pressed.

```
2200 REM Program INKEY.BAS shows a loop to check for any key
pressed
2300 PRINT "Press any key to continue (Q to quit)"
2400 C$=INKEY$:IF C$="Q" OR C$="q" THEN LOOP1=0
2450 IF C$="" GOTO 2400
2500 CLS:END
```

MARYSONG.BAS

"Mary Had a Little Lamb," played by BASIC.

```
5 REM MARYSONG.BAS Plays Mary Had a Little Lamb
10 PLAY "O3 E D C D E E L2E L4D D L2D L4E G L2G"
20 PLAY "L4E D C D E E E E D D E D L2C."
```

OCEAN.BAS

This ocean adventure shows you several ways you can build your own programs.

```
10 REM OCEAN.BAS Program about salmon adventure
20 CLS
30 PRINT "You are one of the last few living red salmon."
40 PRINT
```

continues

```
45 PRINT
50 PRINT "You are trying to survive the dangers of your long"
60 PRINT "ocean trek back to the river where you were born."
70 PRINT "You must return there so you can mate and"
80  PRINT "produce a new generation of red salmon."
90  PRINT
100 PRINT
110 PRINT "Along your journey there are many dangers.  Can "
120 PRINT "your species survive another generation?"
130 PRINT
140 PRINT
150 PRINT
160 PRINT
170 PRINT
180 PRINT "To start your next adventure,"
190 PRINT "press any key  (or Q to quit)"
195 CHOICE$ = INKEY$
200 IF CHOICE$ = "" THEN GOTO 195
210 IF CHOICE$ = "Q" OR CHOICE$ = "q" THEN END
220 CLS
300 REM Computer picks next adventure
305 RANDOMIZE (12345)
310 ADVENTURE = INT(6 * RND(1)) + 1
320 IF ADVENTURE = 1 THEN GOTO 1000
330 IF ADVENTURE = 2 THEN GOTO 2000
340 IF ADVENTURE = 3 THEN GOTO 3000
350 IF ADVENTURE = 4 THEN GOTO 4000
360 IF ADVENTURE = 5 THEN GOTO 5000
370 IF ADVENTURE = 6 THEN GOTO 6000
1000 REM Bears
1010 PRINT "Bears eat salmon, you know!"
1020 PRINT
1030 PRINT "(You can supply your own adventure story from here...)"
1040 PRINT
1900 GOTO 180
2000 REM Dam
2010 PRINT "There is a dam in your way... what will you do?"
2020 PRINT
2030 PRINT "(You can supply your own adventure story from here...)"
2040 PRINT
2900 GOTO 180
3000 REM Pollution
```

```
3010 PRINT "AAAGGGH, what is that nasty, gooey gunky stuff in the water?"
3020 PRINT "It may be an oil slick!"
3030 PRINT
3040 PRINT "(You can supply your own adventure story from here...)"
3050 PRINT
3900 GOTO 180
4000 REM Bigger Fish
4010 PRINT "You see a much larger fish up ahead. Is he hungry?"
4020 PRINT
4030 PRINT "(You can supply your own adventure story from here...)"
4040 PRINT
4900 GOTO 180
5000 REM Scientists
5010 PRINT "The scientists in the submarine will not hurt you..."
5020 PRINT
5030 PRINT "(You can supply your own adventure story from here...)"
5040 PRINT
5900 GOTO 180
6000 REM Ocean
6010 PRINT "You can just barely make out the sunlight"
6020 PRINT "streaming through the blue-green ocean above."
6025 PRINT
6030 PRINT "Suddenly, you see a yellow submarine research station,"
6040 PRINT "where scientists are studying this secret world"
6050 PRINT "beneath the waves. "
6055 PRINT
6060 PRINT
6070 PRINT "(Press any key to continue)"
6075 WHILE INKEY$ = "": WEND
6080 PRINT "Watch out! A net brushes by your right fin.  It could"
6090 PRINT "belong to fishermen, ready to put you into a can"
6100 PRINT "for the grocery.  Up ahead you see a human in scuba"
6110 PRINT "gear.  Are they dangerous?"
6120 PRINT
6200 PRINT
6210 PRINT "DO YOU:"
6220 PRINT "1) Stay put so the scuba diver doesn't see you?"
6230 PRINT "2) Turn around and swim like crazy?"
6250 PRINT "Type in your choice and press ENTER"
6260 INPUT N
6270 IF N = 2 THEN GOTO 6500
6290 IF N <> 1 THEN GOTO 6210
6300 REM CHOICE1
6310 PRINT "The net catches several fish to your right."
```

continues

```
6320 PRINT "By staying calm, you avoid the net as it "
6330 PRINT "passes under you.  Phew, that was close!"
6340 PRINT
6350 PRINT "(Press any key to continue)"
6360 WHILE INKEY$ = "": WEND
6370 REM End of CHOICE1
6380 GOTO 180
6500 REM CHOICE2
6505 CLS
6510 PRINT "As you turn around, your tail gets caught"
6520 PRINT "in the net. You struggle to free yourself, but"
6530 PRINT "you feel yourself being pulled through the water."
6540 PRINT
6550 PRINT "(Press any key to continue)"
6560 WHILE INKEY$ = "": WEND
6570 PRINT
6580 PRINT "To make matters worse, here comes the scuba diver,"
6590 PRINT "carrying a knife. Oh no, it looks like this is it"
6600 PRINT "for you."
6610 PRINT
6620 PRINT "(Press any key to continue)"
6630 WHILE INKEY$ = "": WEND
6640 PRINT "But wait! The scuba diver is not stabbing at"
6650 PRINT "you!  She is cutting the net away. You are "
6660 PRINT "free. That was a close call."
6670 REM End of choice2
6680 GOTO 180
```

OCTAVE.BAS

This program plays musical notes, both with and without the commands that change the octave.

```
2 REM OCTAVE.BAS Shows what happens when < and > are used
3 REM to show which octave to play
5 REM This line does not tell which octave to use
10 REM  "C D E F G A B C D E F G A B C D E F G "
15 REM This line tells which octave to use
20 REM PLAY "O2 C D E F G A B >C D E F G A B >C D E F G "
25 REM the next line plays the same line as 20
30 PLAY "O2 C D E F G A B O3 C D E F G A B O4 C D E F G "
```

OCTCOLOR.BAS

This program draws an octopus.

```
100 REM Program: OCTCOLOR.BAS (Demonstrates SCREEN 1 statements)
200 REM
300 GOSUB 1000        'Housekeeping:
400 GOSUB 3400        'Draw octopus:
500 GOSUB 1700        'Background of ocean and waves
700 GOTO 10800        'End routine
800 REM *****subroutines******
900 REM
1000 REM Housekeeping:
1100 REM DIM IMAGE(8000)        'Dimension storage array
1200 KEY OFF
1300 SCREEN 1                   'Select GRAPHICS
1400 COLOR 0                    'Background color of ocean
1500 CLS
1600 RETURN
1700 REM *********************************************
1800 REM Background:
1900 REM Wave A
2000 FOR WAVE = 250 TO 300 STEP 25
2100     CIRCLE (WAVE, 20), 12, 1, PI, 0, .5
2200 NEXT WAVE
2300 REM Wave B
2400 FOR WAVE = 250 TO 300 STEP 25
2500     CIRCLE (WAVE, 150), 12, 1, PI, 0, .5
2600 NEXT WAVE
2700 REM Wave C
2800 FOR WAVE = 25 TO 75 STEP 25
2900     CIRCLE (WAVE, 120), 12, 1, PI, 0, .5
3000 NEXT WAVE
3300 RETURN
3400 REM *********************************************
3500 REM Draw octopus:
3600        PI = 4 * ATN(1) 'Calculate value of PI
c3700 REM Outline of Head
3800        CIRCLE (150, 60), 60, , 10 * PI / 6, 8 * PI / 6, 2
3900 REM Eyes
4000        CIRCLE (155, 95), 5
4100        CIRCLE (145, 95), 5
4200 REM arms
```

continues

```
4300 REM Each arm needs two partial circles
4400 REM BOTTOM ARM ON RIGHT
4500       CIRCLE (170, 125), 12, , PI / 2, 3 * PI / 2, 1
4600       CIRCLE (170, 150), 12, , 3 * PI / 2, PI / 2, 1
4700 REM BOTTOM ARM ON LEFT
4800       CIRCLE (145, 125), 12, , PI / 2, 3 * PI / 2, 1
4900       CIRCLE (145, 150), 12, , 3 * PI / 2, PI / 2, 1
5000 REM ARM ON RIGHT STRAIGHT OUT
5100       CIRCLE (200, 100), 12, , 0, PI
5200       CIRCLE (224, 100), 12, , PI, 0
5300 REM ARM ON LEFT STRAIGHT OUT
5400       CIRCLE (100, 100), 12, , 0, PI
5500       CIRCLE (76, 100), 12, , PI, 0
5600 REM ARM ON RIGHT TOP
5700       CIRCLE (200, 75), 12, , PI / 6, PI
5800       CIRCLE (217, 60), 12, , 2.5 * PI / 2, PI / 6
5900 REM ARM ON LEFT TOP
6000       CIRCLE (100, 75), 12, , 0, 5 * PI / 6
6100       CIRCLE (83, 60), 12, , 5 * PI / 6, 1.75 * PI
6200 REM ARM ANGLED DOWN AND RIGHT
6300       CIRCLE (175, 120), 20, , 11 * PI / 6, PI / 2, .6
6400       CIRCLE (203, 135), 15, , 4 * PI / 6, 1.75 * PI, 1
6500 REM ARM ANGLED DOWN AND LEFT
6600       CIRCLE (115, 120), 20, , PI / 3, 7 * PI / 6, .6
6700       CIRCLE (93, 133), 12, , 7 * PI / 6, PI / 3, .6
6800 GOSUB 9800          'Eyebrows:
7100 RETURN
9800 REM ************************************************
9900 REM Eyebrows:
10000 REM Angry
10100 REM PSET (150, 92)  'Position for next DRAW statements
10200 REM DRAW "BE5 E5 BG10 BH5 H5"  'Angry
10300 REM    'Worried
10400     PSET (150, 65)        'Position for next DRAW statements
10500     DRAW " BF5 F5 BH10 BG5 G5"     'Worried
10600     PRESET (150, 65)   'Hide the point
10700 RETURN
10800 REM End routine ****************************************
10900 END
```

PETE.BAS

This is the "Pete and Repeat" riddle in a program.

```
10   REM Program PETE.BAS  (Program to repeat a riddle)
20   CLS
30   PRINT "Bobby: Hey, Kevin! Try to guess the right answer!"
40   FOR COUNT% = 1 TO 3
50       PRINT "Bobby: Pete and Repeat sat on a fence."
60       PRINT "       Pete fell off and who was left?"
70       PRINT "Kevin: Repeat?"
80       PRINT "Bobby: OK..."
85       PRINT
90   NEXT COUNT%
100  PRINT "Kevin: I get it, now.  Very funny!"
110  PRINT "       Let's get some ice cream now!"
120  END
```

SCALE.BAS

This musical program demonstrates sharp and flat keys.

```
5 REM SCALE.BAS plays musical scales to demonstrate sharps and
   flats
10 PLAY "O4 C    D    E F    G    A    B > C" 'White keys only
20 PLAY "O4 C C+ D D+ E F F+ G G+ A A+ B > C" 'Black and white keys
30 PLAY "O4 C D- D E- E F G- G A- A B- B > C" 'Black and white keys
```

SLIME.BAS

This program is the slime monster adventure.

```
5    REM SLIME.BAS Slime monster adventure
10   CLS
20   PRINT "You are skateboarding along your favorite section of
     sidewalk"
30   PRINT "when you hear a gooey, drippy slime monster at your
     side."
40   PRINT
50   PRINT "Think fast!"
60   REM The following section shows player the possible choices
```

continues

```
70   PRINT
80   PRINT "DO YOU"
90   PRINT "(1) CHOOSE TO TURN AND FACE THE MUTANT? "
100  PRINT "(2) CONTINUE ON YOUR RIDE?"
110  PRINT "(3) RUN AWAY?"
120  PRINT "TYPE IN YOUR CHOICE AND PRESS ENTER"
130  INPUT CHOICE
140  IF CHOICE = 2 THEN GOTO 210
150  IF CHOICE = 3 THEN GOTO 260
160  IF CHOICE <> 1 THEN GOTO 60
170  REM CHOICE1: FACE MUTANT
180  PRINT "Congratulations on your courage. The slime monster
       slithers away"
190  PRINT "when it sees how mad you are."
200  END
210  REM CHOICE 2: CONTINUE ON PATH
220  PRINT "As you ride away, the slime monster lands a water
       balloon"
230  PRINT "right on your head. It is a hot day, and it feels
       pretty"
240  PRINT "good, actually. You are safe, for the time being."
250  END
260  REM CHOICE 3: RUN AWAY
270  PRINT "The slime monster thinks you are a big chicken. He is
       faster than"
280  PRINT "you are. He grabs you and pulls your favorite pair"
290  PRINT "of purple high tops right off of your feet."
300  PRINT "You are safe for the time being, but your mother is
       going "
310  PRINT "to kill you when you get home for losing those shoes!"
320  END
```

WORM.BAS

This program draws a worm using graphics, and then adds more using ASCII characters.

```
10  REM Program: WORM.BAS (Uses CIRCLE and DRAW statements)
15  REM Also uses ASCII characters for antennas
20  SCREEN 2     'Select high-resolution graphics
30  CLS
50  PI = 4 * ATN(1)
55  REM Draw body of worm
```

```
60 FOR COUNT = 1 TO 200 STEP 25
65 X = 300 + COUNT
70 CIRCLE (X, 100), 18, , PI / 4, 3.5 * PI / 2        'Shape C
80 NEXT COUNT
85 REM Draw Head
90 CIRCLE (X, 100), 18
100 REM Draw eyes
110 REM Position left eye
120 LEFT = X - 3
130 CIRCLE (LEFT, 97), 2
140 RIGHT = X + 6
150 CIRCLE (RIGHT, 97), 2
160 REM Draw smile
170 REM Go back to center of head
180 CIRCLE (X, 100), 10, , 1.25 * PI, 1.75 * PI
185 LOCATE 12, 59
190 PRINT CHR$(41); " "; CHR$(40)
```

YESNO.BAS

This is the subroutine from 8BALLSUB.BAS. It asks a yes-or-no question, and then gets the answer from the player.

```
5   REM Progam YESNO.BAS  (Routine for yes-or-no question)
10 PRINT "Would you like to ask the all-knowing 8-Ball a question?"
20 PRINT "Type in Y for yes, or N for no, then press ENTER"
30 INPUT YESNO$
40 REM Don't let the player enter anything but Y,y,N,n
50 IF YESNO$ = "y" OR YESNO$ = "Y" THEN GOTO 440
60 IF YESNO$ = "n" THEN GOTO 390
70 IF YESNO$ <> "N" THEN 20
```

INDEX

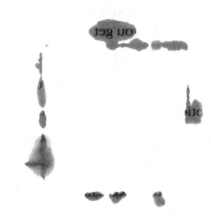

Join the Alpha Kids Club Today!

The coolest computer users join the Alpha Kids club. When you become a member of Alpha Kids, you get a membership kit with a membership card. You also get:

- An 800 telephone number to use if you need help with *Building with BASIC*.
- A subscription to *Kids Computer Forum*, the quarterly club newsletter.
- Alpha Kids disk labels, so you can keep track of your floppy disks.
- Other neat surprises!

And — here's the most excellent part — joining Alpha Kids is FREE!!! Just fill in and mail the card below.

ALPHA KIDS DISK EXCHANGE

IF YOUR COMPUTER USES 3½" DISKS

While many personal computers use 5¼" disks to store information, some newer computers use 3½" disks. If your IBM-compatible computer uses 3½" disks, return the form below to Alpha Books and we will send you a 3½" disk to use with this book. YOU DO NOT HAVE TO ENROLL YOUR CHILD IN THE ALPHA KIDS CLUB TO REQUEST A 3½" DISK.

Print the required information on this reply form and mail it to:

ALPHA KIDS/DISK EXCHANGE

a
alpha books

A Division of Prentice Hall Computer Publishing
11711 North College, Carmel, Indiana 46032 USA

Name: _____

Address: _____

City: _____ State: ____ ZIP: _____

Work phone: _____ Home: _____

—— Please send me a 3½" *Building with BASIC* disk

—— Please enroll my child (children) in the Alpha Kids Club.

Name _____

_____ Boy _____ Girl

Age _____ Birthday _____

Name _____

_____ Boy _____ Girl

Age _____ Birthday _____

Note: Membership is free.